Dot
& Ralfie

Also by Amy Hoffman

The Off Season

Lies About My Family

An Army of Ex-Lovers: My Life at the Gay Community News

Hospital Time

Dot
& Ralfie

AMY HOFFMAN

THE UNIVERSITY OF WISCONSIN PRESS

The University of Wisconsin Press
728 State Street, Suite 443
Madison, Wisconsin 53706
uwpress.wisc.edu

Gray's Inn House, 127 Clerkenwell Road
London EC1R 5DB, United Kingdom
eurospanbookstore.com

Printed in the United States of America
This book may be available in a digital edition.

Library of Congress Cataloging-in-Publication Data

Names: Hoffman, Amy, author.
Title: Dot & Ralfie / Amy Hoffman.
Other titles: Dot and Ralfie
Description: Madison, Wisconsin : The University of Wisconsin Press, [2022]
Identifiers: LCCN 2021038690 | ISBN 9780299333645 (paperback)
Subjects: LCSH: Older lesbians—Fiction. | LCGFT: Fiction. | Novels.
Classification: LCC PS3608.O47738 D68 2022 | DDC 813/.6—dc23
LC record available at https://lccn.loc.gov/2021038690

This is a work of fiction. All names, characters, places, and incidents are either
products of the author's imagination or are used fictitiously.

Contents

Dot
& Ralfie

I

There's Ralfie

There's Ralfie. She's stuck on the living room couch, wearing her safety-orange Boston Department of Public Works hoody and a huge pair of pink satin boxers decorated with red hearts, a joke gift from Dot last Valentine's, but they're easier to pull on over her knee brace than anything else in her dresser, and she likes the feeling of the slick material against her bare butt. She twitches back and forth a couple of times, and an image flashes briefly in her head: dancing at the bar back in the day, agile, sexy, taking up with one girl, then another, her crewcut, which is now gray, still dark. Pumping her fists in the air, clapping her hands above her head. *Uh-huh, uh-huh.* She could *move.* Now her right leg is dutifully elevated on a couple of bed pillows piled on the coffee table, and she's wielding the TV clicker like a gun. If only she could blast the thing right in the screen. Not a goddamn thing on.

She had woken from the surgery to see the doc standing over her, a serious expression plastered on his face. "Just like we told you, your knee was a mess," he said. He was still wearing his green scrubs. She and Dot had chosen him because he seemed so experienced and confident, but with the cap hiding his considerable bald spot, he looked barely old enough to have graduated medical school.

"A mess," said Ralfie. "So that's the term of art?"

He had chuckled and rubbed his manicured hands together. "In layman's terms, yeah. Complicated procedure. Give it three-four months and a course of PT, you'll be good as new." And that was about all the information she and Dot ever got out of him. The days in rehab, the crawl to their third-floor flat when Ralfie was finally deposited back home—none of that, the nurses explained, was a doctor's concern.

Now her leg is throbbing, her water glass is empty, and her pain pills are next to the bathroom sink. They might as well be in Siberia. "Hey, Dot!" she yells, pointlessly. "You suck!" Dot, an elementary school librarian, is at work. It's not even lunchtime. Of course Ralfie would never yell at Dot like that if Dot could actually hear her. Dot's a saint.

Ralfie picks up her leg and lowers it carefully onto the floor, leans across the couch to reach her crutches, tucks them under her armpits, hops slowly across Siberia to the bathroom. Balances while she shakes a few painkillers into her palm, dry swallows them, hops back to the couch. She's lying across it when Dot gets home, out cold, arms crossed over her chest, head thrown back, snorting and wheezing.

Dot shakes her by the shoulder. "How many pills did you take?"

Ralfie opens one eye and shrugs. "Not enough," she says. "Give us a kiss."

Dot's gone over to the closet to hang up her coat, but she purses her lips and aims a few kisses back at Ralfie, who opens the other eye. "You suck, Dot," she says, pushing herself up to sit. "I meant a real kiss." She heaves her leg onto the pillow arrangement on the coffee table, pats the couch next to her.

Dot sits down and puts her arm around Ralfie's shoulder. "How was your day, baby?"

"Sucked. Yours?"

"A kid peed all over the floor back in the middle-grade stacks. We only noticed it after story circle."

"But nobody threw up."

"Nope, nobody threw up."

"So, all in all, pretty good."

"Not bad. We made the grad student clean it up. Part of his training."

2

So There's Dot

So there's Dot. Dot's girlfriend—she never thinks of Ralfie as her wife, it just doesn't feel natural—is recovering from a knee replacement after resisting the surgery for years, and in Dot's opinion, she's behaving like a child over it, taking the pain pills, drowning her sorrows. Dot hadn't expected that, because after all Ralfie gets bashed up constantly—on the job, playing Tuesday basketball. That's what finally did in her knee: showing off some move she saw on television. She jumps! She twists! She yelps and goes down spectacularly, and her teammates gather around her shouting instructions. "Help me get her up!" "No, don't move her!" EMTs appear and haul her off the court on a stretcher.

Also, if it was Dot, she would be stoic. She knows this about herself. Her knee throbs too, and sometimes she gets strange aches in her muscles, but she doesn't mention these to anyone, nor does she complain about Ralfie's pill popping, not even on the phone to Susan. Her younger sister, Susan, doesn't get Ralfie, or refuses to, even after all this time, and Dot isn't up for yet another debate: "I just don't see the appeal, Dorothy." "Don't call me Dorothy." Etcetera. Susan only says *Dorothy* when she's in busybody mode, evaluating Dot's relationships, her job, her dinner plans, whatever. The two are a contrast: Dot willowy, sandy-haired, with a face that's always seemed to her—although not to anyone else—just a bit too long; Susan short and stocky, with curly black hair. They don't look like sisters, but that's DNA for you. In fact, Dot is more often mistaken for Ralfie's sibling than Susan's, although she resembles Ralfie even less than she does her actual sister. It happens all the time to lesbian couples. The straights sense the connection, but they can't quite identify it.

Dot made the mistake of confiding to Susan that there's a second knee replacement in Ralfie's future, although Dot and Ralfie themselves have

5

managed not to have a conversation about it. Ralfie's ortho sat them down to give them the bad news at her last appointment. It brings up too many questions. Like, how long can Ralfie keep up at the DPW? They've tried to promote her off the truck about a million times, but she likes—needs—the variety, filling a pothole, pruning a tree, pulling up the yellow tulips in the square and planting the red, white, and blue petunias, rescuing some old lady's cat off the porch roof before she and the guys knock off for the day. And being outside in all weathers, flexing her muscles, rocking her safety-orange sweatshirt and her steel-toed boots. She would shrivel behind a desk, and Ralfie shriveled, Dot can predict, would be no picnic.

Dot offers, "Dinner, my dear? How about a lovely black bean casserole?" They don't eat that way anymore, although sometimes Dot wishes they would just go veg, it's so much healthier, and they would probably both lose weight, which they could definitely afford to do, especially Ralfie, with her knees. It's been quite a while since she was the slip of the thing Dot had first met.

Ralfie growls, "Meeeat, meeeat."

"Burger?"

Ralfie pants and nods enthusiastically.

"You nut." When the food is ready, Dot brings their plates to the couch, and they eat in front of the TV—a big one, equipped by Ralfie with every sports station imaginable, the more expensive the better. They've been known to do this even when Ralfie hasn't just had surgery. Dot likes a good old black-and-white movie, something with a plot to it, but Ralfie, predictably, insists on the Patriots.

3

The Only Thing to Live For

The physical therapist is maybe the only thing Ralfie has to live for anymore, which isn't saying much. That, and Dot's appearance in the evening, when they snuggle and schmooze on the couch for fifteen, twenty minutes before one of them gets up to make dinner. Or, that's how it used to be—a sweet interval, and then they took turns with the cooking. Ralfie had her specialties, Dot had hers. Now it's all fallen on Dot, and when she runs out of ideas, they have corn flakes. Breakfast for dinner. Ralfie would never stoop to that. She would at least scramble some eggs, grate up some cheese. Serve them with ketchup for Dot, hot sauce for her, enough to make her feel like she's breathing fire.

Ralfie's not a bad cook, she compliments herself, remembering a woman she had seduced over a bottle of red wine and her old nonna's *bistecca*. You marinate it in Paul Newman's Italian dressing, and to get a good sear disconnect the smoke alarms. Her nonna would have served pasta on the side, but Ralfie, figuring her date was watching her waistline—they all were—had made a green salad instead. Torn lettuce leaves, a sprinkle of the dressing, some shavings off a block of parmesan, the real kind, from Italy—none of that stuff from the green can, which Ralfie's puzzled nonna had concluded wasn't cheese at all but tiny pellets of plastic left over from the manufacture of styrofoam. Ralfie hadn't bothered with dessert, she knew they wouldn't get that far. In fact, they didn't even finish the steaks, expensive as they were—but worth the money. Eating isn't everything, Ralfie thinks—and her nonna would have agreed. The old girl had been a real pistol, and Ralfie was named for her, Rafaela, although even as they christened her, bawling, squirming, grabbing her little lace bonnet and hurling it to the floor to reveal a head full of wiry black hair, the priest, her parents, and the entire gathered congregation had realized the pretty name would never fit this kid.

As usual the therapist rings the doorbell, which Ralfie finds utterly annoying, since she can't get down the stairs to answer it, and she's given the therapist a key. "Come on up!" she yells.

The therapist, Shelly, appears in the doorway. "Good morning, Ms. Ralfie!" She's a cheery type, so far undeflatable, as much as Ralfie pricks her.

Ralfie doesn't return the greeting. "Why do you have to ring that bell all the time?"

"We're not supposed to take our clients by surprise," explains Shelly. She's only a few years out of school, earnest, still rehearsing what she's learned.

"Because I could be doing anything up here, you mean?" says Ralfie, trying to look lewd.

Shelly doesn't respond, but a blush spreads up her face. "Let's get to work!"

Ralfie, feeling she's gotten herself on top of the situation, reaches for her crutches. "This therapy is just walking around. I do that anyway. I don't know what I need you for."

"The company?" says Shelly, trying to coax her into a better mood.

"Could be worse," Ralfie concedes. And really if Shelly weren't there, Ralfie would be spending yet another day totally bored, zonked on painkillers. "Okay, let's do this."

As Shelly observes her, Ralfie stumps around the apartment on her crutches, then at Shelly's instruction, lies on the couch and does a few leg lifts, points and flexes her foot, movements that in normal times she wouldn't consider exercise at all. With the knee, though, they're killers.

"Awesome! Working hard!" Shelly babbles. "It really is too bad about all those stairs. With this knee, and then the other, they're not going to get any easier."

"Who said anything about the other knee?"

"Your record. It says the doc talked to you—"

"Just shut up about that," says Ralfie, glaring at her.

"It's not like it's my fault!"

"Oh no?" says Ralfie, irrationally. She knows she's being ridiculous, but she wishes there were someone to blame. It just seems so wrong for her, Ralfie Santopietro, of all people, to be in this situation, limping around, needing a hand from Dot even to lower herself onto the toilet, for chris-sake. There hasn't been a week since she quit business school when she hasn't gone to the gym at least a couple of days. And run, in all weathers—you just have to know how to dress. Fleece. And when the temperature goes below forty, a Pats ski hat with a big red pompom.

"You're right, one thing at a time," says Shelly. "Let's do another set of the leg lifts."

"What do you mean, *let's*," Ralfie says. "I don't see you doing anything." She had always figured she would go all at once. Massive coronary in her sleep, like that. Unfortunately her cholesterol and blood pressure are great, and she's got no family history, at least as far as anyone's been able to tell her, although who knows what those crazy *paisans* were getting up to back in Napoli. So she's *too* healthy. With the bionic knees she'll probably have to quit running, so that will be one strike against her. Her sudden death would be hard on Dot, she thinks with a shudder of guilt, but slow disinte-gration—that could be worse.

4

Not a Good Time

At the library, Dot gets a call from Susan. It's not a good time. The first-graders will be arriving any minute to choose their reading for the week, and Dot's laying out a selection of picture books on the low tables when her cell phone rings. Worried that it's some sort of Ralfie emergency, she picks up.

"I have to tell you about this idea Germaine had over the weekend! We went to Ogunquit, you know, up to Maine, for a little six-month anniversary. Already, can you believe it? Even after all this time, I still think she's *so hot*. I think she could really be the one, Dotty, you know? Not just because of the fantastic sex. She's a good person, always thinking of others. So we're coming down 95 and there's this sign for a condo development, and we took the exit . . ."

Ralfie had offered to program Dot's phone to play a different chime for each caller, but Dot hadn't seen the point. Now she wishes she had allowed Ralfie to fiddle with it; she could have screened Susan out. Dot has met Germaine only a couple of times, when she didn't see evidence of her exceptional goodness and empathy—although she has to agree with Susan that Germaine is adorable, in the gamine style: no tits, no hips, huge dark eyes that she probably exaggerates with makeup, always wearing a hat, which she shouldn't get away with but somehow does. Lately, befitting her identity as a proud Quebecoise, it's a beret. Her English, Dot suspects, is completely fluent, but she's cultivated such a twisted accent that Dot can make out only about half of her conversation, and she suspects the same is true for Susan. "I can't talk now. This place is going to be overrun with children any second. I'll call you on my lunch break."

"No, don't," says Susan. "I have a client."

Susan is a life coach, whatever that is. She also counsels formerly homeless women who have moved into apartments, helping them get back on their feet, a vocation Dot admires her for. Others who attempt it find the women's endless problems disheartening and quickly burn out, but it's exactly the job for Susan. She loves tinkering with the women's lives—organizing their budgets, finding them psychotherapists, accompanying them to court, visiting them in the hospital, sending them off to Weight Watchers and Alcoholics Anonymous. At her agency she's a star, but they can only afford to pay her half time, thus the life coaching—which, Susan has explained to Dot, is kind of the same, except she can charge an arm and a leg for it.

"And you have to hear this *now*, it's brilliant," Susan continues.

"Isn't Germaine, like, ten years younger than you?"

"Fifteen. But Dot, it doesn't matter. That's the thing."

Led by their teacher, the first-graders come marching through the door two by two, holding hands. They're so unbearably cute, sometimes Dot wishes she could just, oh, pick one up, tuck her under her arm, and take her home. Or, strangely, weep—and not because she's ever wanted kids of her own. That's not her shtick. She knows the theory: their big eyes and little noses and all that. And they're just so—miniature. Dot towers over them—over their teacher, too. She was the girl in the middle of the back row in the class picture, flanked by boys shorter than her. She's never tried to mitigate her height; her posture is like a dancer's, and today, for fun, she's wearing her hair piled high on top of her head and held together with a yellow pencil, as a librarian ought, a pair of cat-eye readers hanging around her neck, although she doesn't need them. Much. The children scatter around the tables, chattering, and the teacher reminds them, "What do we do in the library?" putting her finger to her lips. They imitate her, giggling and whispering loudly, and Dot's eyes start to burn.

"I'm hanging up," she chokes out. "Later, okay?" But she's already decided not to call back. She really does not want to hear Germaine's brilliant idea, especially since she suspects she knows what it is. She's seen that sign on 95 too, pointing toward the exit for a condo development especially designed for adults "55 or better." Germaine probably figures Dot and Ralfie are decrepit enough to need locking away.

Dot gets home to discover that Susan's been at Ralfie too, calling her when she couldn't get Dot to pick up the phone again, and Ralfie's hopping mad. Literally. She's so agitated she can't sit still, and since she can't exactly pace, she's been crutching in circles around the living room, carving divots in the rug. Dot's almost grateful, though—it's better than finding her passed out on the couch. More like the normal Ralfie. "Your sister's got a nerve!" Ralfie fumes. "Her and that Canadian twit she brought around here. Who do they think they are?"

So Dot guessed right about the sign. "Uh-huh," she says.

"What? And she said *you* think it's a good idea!"

"Susan will say anything! She called me at work, but I was busy."

"They want to put us in an old-age home! Because of my knees. I'd like to bop them in the knees!" It's such a Three Stooges thing to come out with, Ralfie stops and snorts, momentarily laughs at herself.

"It's not exactly an old-age home," says Dot. But that revs Ralfie up again.

"See, Susan was right. You *are* into it!"

"I'm not! But it's not an old-age home. It's just a condo development."

"We already have a condo!"

"Exactly," says Dot, worried that the usual underground tension between Susan and Ralfie is about to break into the open. "Stop yelling. Susan was just trying to help."

"Some help," says Ralfie. "Can you see us in the burbs? Me, working on my golf swing?"

"You like golf," Dot points out. She refuses to even try it, walking an arid course in the unrelenting sun. She would much rather wait in the air-conditioned club house, with a good book and a cold drink, a light sweater draped over her shoulders.

"When I play with the guys! They're not going to go all the way up there. Anyway, look at me. I'd have to get a cart. They'd laugh."

"Aw, baby," says Dot. "Come here. No one's laughing."

5

An Expedition

It becomes an expedition. For the first time, Ralfie manages to bump herself down the front stairs on her butt with hardly any help from Dot, which, Ralfie proudly explains, is an accomplishment: it takes a surprising amount of arm strength. They drive around to pick up first Susan and then Germaine, who rushes out her door carrying a basket she's packed with sandwiches, a couple of Cokes, cut-up oranges, an ice pack, napkins. She's not nearly as much of a twit as Dot and Ralfie think, and she's been taking English conversation classes twice a week. "After the tour, a *pique-nique!*" she announces.

"Darling!" says Susan. "How sweet!"

"Kind of cold for that, though, isn't it?" says Ralfie.

"We will find some nice place," Germaine enunciates. "Maybe in the *community room*! I saw on the website. Very pretty, and for all to use."

"Old-age homes have websites?" says Ralfie.

"Condo developments." Dot sighs. "And we're just looking, remember?"

Germaine looks puzzled. "Everybody has websites," she says. "*Naturellement.*"

They pull up to a low beige building, a shoe box, basically, that matches those in the office park next door—except for the main entrance, which has an imposing, pillared portico.

"No, over there," Ralfie corrects Dot, who's aiming for Visitor Parking. Ralfie points her to the handicapped space in front of the door instead.

"Hey!" says Germaine. "Not fair! The disabled, they need it."

"And?" says Ralfie, extricating a permit from the glove box and hanging it on the rear-view mirror. "I'm a cripple, that's why we're here, remember?"

A woman comes out of the building, waving at them exaggeratedly. She's probably in her late sixties, like Dot and Ralfie, but she looks like she belongs to another generation. Middle-aged straight ladies always do, Dot muses—although as they get older and lose their husbands, they can't be bothered to dye and style their hair anymore; they bob it short and pad around in sneakers and jeans, and at a certain point, they and the lesbians all look the same. Their greeter hasn't gotten to that point. Her body is sort of rectangular, and she's wearing a wool skirt and actual hose. Pearls and a twin set. Dot wouldn't be surprised to find out she's got on a girdle, holding it all together, although of course she will never get the chance to confirm that.

Waiting for them to pile out of the car, the woman smiles broadly, her mouth outlined in vermilion. "Welcome, welcome!" she calls. "Welcome to Maple Grove—and we do have maples, you know. Quite venerable ones! They made sure to keep them when they built the townhouses. We're not like those places, Mountainview Lakes or whatever, that are miles from any lake or mountain." She laughs at her little joke. "Our grounds here are just lovely in the fall. I always say you can go leaf-peeping right from your own kitchen window—while some people have to travel miles and miles."

Susan introduces them. "Susan Greenbaum," she says with a nod. "My sister, Dorothy Greenbaum," she continues, putting an affectionate arm around Dot."

"Dot," says Dot, shaking off Susan's hand. She doesn't let just anyone call her Dorothy.

Ignoring her, Susan finishes. "And this is Germaine Belrose. And our Ralfie." As though everybody has one.

"Ah." The woman nods, as though these introductions explain something. "Mrs. Dailey." She extends her hand, and Ralfie reaches over her crutches to shake it. Mrs. Dailey takes it hesitantly. She's trying to figure out the relationships among this tour group. "Mr. Belrose," she concludes. "Aren't you the lucky one, surrounded by all these pretty ladies."

Ralfie's been mistaken for a man before, and generally, it's not a situation she wants to get herself into. With younger guys, especially, it can turn dangerous, once they realize their mistake—*you think you're so tough, ya little perv, c'mon over here and prove it.* At first, she would take the dare and fight, but that led inevitably to injury. She prided herself on giving as good as she got, until the night when she ended up in the hospital with a concussion, a couple of black eyes, and three broken ribs, which caused a stabbing pain for months, every time she yawned or sneezed. Never again, she vowed. She became expert at deflecting aggression with humor, especially with new guys on the truck. These days, challenges are rare. Mrs. Dailey, though, has handed Ralfie an irresistible opportunity, and she plays along. "You bet," she growls.

Dot catches her eye, and Ralfie winks. Against Dot's better judgment, she grins back. Susan glares at them but keeps her mouth shut.

Mrs. Dailey leads them through the pillars into the foyer, Dot and Susan in front, Ralfie, who's positioned herself next to Germaine, following. Germaine finds the whole thing uncomfortable, having this strange man sidling up to her while her actual girlfriend has rushed off ahead, but then she reminds herself, it's not a strange man, it's Ralfie.

"Our front desk is staffed twenty-four hours a day," says Mrs. Dailey. "Isn't that right . . . uh . . . ."

"Cynthia," says the woman sitting at the desk, who is dwarfed by an enormous flower arrangement. She's wearing a crisp white shirt with a button-down collar and a navy-and-pink striped tie, an outfit that suggests a uniform, although not that of Maple Grove. Maybe it's the pink. "Absolutely, Mrs. Dailey. We pride ourselves. We take deliveries, arrange their travel."

"Concierge service," says Mrs. Dailey, "is included. Thank you . . . uh . . . Cindy."

"Cyn-thi-a," the concierge enunciates, since this happens almost every day. Ignoring her, Mrs. Dailey nudges the group along to their next stop.

"Impressive," booms Ralfie.

Mrs. Dailey looks at her suspiciously. "We receive a beautiful fresh bouquet every week, Mr. Belrose. Just one of our lovely touches. Now let me show you one of our units."

"Don't you love it?" Susan asks Dot excitedly. "All the parking and that grand foyer and a *concierge*! I thought that was only in France." Susan decides not to mention a weird thing that happened just as they turned to walk down the long hall. It seemed to her that the concierge had caught her eye and given her a little flick of the eyebrows. The concierge's eyebrows, in contrast to her spikey blonde hair, are heavy and dark. But when Susan glanced back, the concierge was looking down, apparently preoccupied, as she swept a few stray petals from her desk into her cupped hand. So, thinks Susan, maybe she imagined it. She looks around for Germaine, but with

Ralfie on crutches, they've fallen behind. "I could live here, Dotty, I really could."

"In a unit," says Dot. "What town are we in again?"

"Oh, please, it doesn't matter. You just shoot down 95 to Boston whenever you want. I could keep my jobs. Hang out with you guys."

"I see," says Dot, nodding at this ridiculous statement. No one shoots down 95. Encircling a city famous for its maniacal drivers and irrational signage—including an Einsteinian stretch on this very highway where you find yourself traveling north and south at the same time—the road is clogged day and night.

Mrs. Dailey produces a rather incongruous, janitorial ring of keys and unlocks one of the many doors lining the hallway. Inside the apartment, Susan admires everything, then reiterates to Dot all the features their guide has just shown them: the granite countertops and silent dishwasher, the waterfall showerhead and gas fireplace. The view is just as promised, a rolling lawn and a stand of large old trees, all of it cleverly landscaped to imply that over the next hill is a Thoreauvian woods rather than an office park.

Back in the living room, Mrs. Dailey stops her guests and arranges them on the armchairs and couches the place has been staged with, all of it unobtrusively tasteful, in neutral shades that can barely be identified as colors. Greige. She switches on the fireplace. "So, that's it!" she says. "What do you think, Mr. Belrose?" Throughout the tour, she's glommed onto Ralfie, having apparently decided she's in charge, and addressed most of her comments to her.

"*Hrmm-hrmm*," Ralfie grunts.

"Oh, enough already, Ralfie!" says Susan, and it dawns on Mrs. Dailey that she's made some sort of error. Susan turns to her. "It's gorgeous," she says. "We're going to have to give this some serious thought."

"Very good," says Mrs. Dailey, less warmly than before, handing around her business cards. "Do call, any of you ladies, if you have any questions whatsoever."

"The community room?" asks Germaine. "Do you know where is that? We brought our lunch."

"I think they have them in some of the other developments, dear. But here we aren't assisted living, you know." Turning off the fireplace, she ushers them out of the building and points to a fork in the path. "That's the shortcut to the parking lot," she says, dismissing them.

"We are in handicapped," says Germaine. "For Ralfie's bad knee."

Mrs. Dailey has been trying not to look at Ralfie, but now she does, and Ralfie gives her a big smile and a wave hello with her crutch. "Same way," says Mrs. Dailey. She's had enough of this group; she doesn't even know anymore whom she's supposed to be selling to. "Just follow it around to the front of the building, and you'll be back where you started."

Exactly, thinks Dot.

6

A Big Waste of Time

"Well, that was a big waste of time," says Ralfie, gnawing on one of Germaine's sandwiches, a French thing with a slice of ham on a hardening baguette. The kid could at least have been a little more generous with the filling, Ralfie thinks, but for a change doesn't say. They were briefly husband and wife, after all.

"Since you're so busy!" says Susan. In the absence of a community room, she invited them all back to her place for the picnic—the better, Dot thinks cynically, to sell them on Maple Grove once she has them on her territory.

"No, no, you were right to arrange it," she tells her sister. "We know a little more now about our alternatives."

"Yeah, right," says Ralfie. "Maple Grave, I call it. Can you see us in there?"

"No," Dot agrees.

"Not another lesbian for miles!" says Ralfie.

"Oh, please, there's got to be a few," says Susan. "Ten percent, right? I could see myself there in a minute!" She surveys her kitchen, which hasn't been updated since the eighties, although the developer at least had the taste to put in white appliances and not the era's harvest gold. "Granite, stainless—and all on one level. You wouldn't have to give your knees another thought."

"Knee," says Ralfie.

"Knee-zzzz," insists Susan. "Knee-zzz. Face facts, would you, for a change!"

"Susan," says Dot. "We're trying. But really, 'Mr. Belrose'?"

"No kidding. I'd have a permanent sore throat from doing that low voice all the time," says Ralfie.

"We'd never fit in," Dot concludes. "And who knows how much it would cost. We didn't even get into that."

"Well, it's too bad," says Susan. She's about to bring up more arguments for Maple Grove, because she's really tempted. She can just see herself and Germaine sitting by the gas fire with mugs of spiced cider she's simmered in that nice kitchen, or barbecuing out on the deck in the summer, the leaves fluttering in a gentle breeze—was there a deck? In any case, she wants to see the place again. If she moved up there, she would want Dot to come along . . .

"And look at you and Germaine." Dot interrupts her reverie, because at certain moments she can read Susan's mind. "They'd think she's your daughter!"

"But that is impossible!" says Germaine.

Susan goes over to where Germaine is sitting, hugs her from behind, buries her face in her neck. "Not a chance," she mumbles. "You're my sweet *cherie*-boo."

"Uh-oh, cherry-boo," Ralfie says. "I think it's time for us to get going, Old Dot."

"Old Ralfie." Dot hands her the crutches, and Ralfie leans on the table to stand, tucks the crutches under her arms, and starts toward the door. "You're getting pretty good at that," says Dot.

"Practice," says Ralfie. "Soon I'll be mountain climbing."

"Mmm," says Germaine as Susan slips her hands under Germaine's T-shirt and starts feeling up her breasts.

"See you later," Dot calls over to them. "Thanks for the sandwiches."

Susan looks up. "Okay, later."

"Oh, baby," says Germaine as Dot and Ralfie walk out the door, and Susan gets down to business.

7

Who Knows Where

Who knows where Susan first encountered Germaine—on the internet, probably, although Dot doesn't quite understand how that works—but here's how Dot and Ralfie met: decades ago, before everyone went online and the bars closed down. Back then you had to physically leave home to meet anyone, so even though Dot wasn't exactly the bar-dyke type, she would turn up on an occasional Friday night, and there she noticed Ralfie, buttoned into a pin-striped skirt-suit, with a vest, and one of those floppy career-girl bows ambitious women used to wear instead of a tie. You never saw such a dyke-in-a-dress as Ralfie in her business school days. She had her outfits beautifully tailored but somehow they never looked it; instead she always looked like she was about to bust right out of them. And indeed, later in the evening the pussy bow would be lost, or tied around Ralfie's head, the shirttails hanging out of the pencil skirt, the sleeves rolled up, the kitten heels kicked off under a barstool. Unbuttoned, Ralfie would be shooting pool in her stocking feet, clobbering one comer after another.

On impulse one Friday, Dot put her name on the list. At her turn, she chose a cue and rubbed the tip with the blue chalk cube as she had seen others do. Leaned down and squinted over the white ball. Slid the cue back and forth between her fingers a couple of times. Scratched, totally. She picked up the ball from the floor next to Ralfie's foot, noticed that the woman's second toe was longer than the big one, which was supposed to mean something, she thought. Good at sex, something like that.

"What the fuck," said Ralfie. "Haven't you done this before?"

"Teach me," said Dot.

"Buy us a beer first," said Ralfie.

But even with the beer, Ralfie quickly got bored with Dot's lack of skill and began glancing over Dot's shoulder toward the dancers in the next room. Finally she put down her cue and wandered off. Ralfie doesn't have the self-reflectiveness of an educator-type like Dot—the memory of what it felt like not to be able to do the thing you now do without thinking, and the steps you took to learn it. So Dot has never learned to shoot pool. One more lesbian life skill she lacks, she jokes. She can't drive a stick either—although she could figure it out, and many more things, too, if she needed to, and that's the difference between youth and age. Back then, standing deserted next to the pool table, watching Ralfie flirt with seemingly every girl in the bar but her, Dot had concluded she was simply incapable.

Ralfie denies the whole episode. As proof, she points out that she would never even have considered shooting pool with Dot, because everybody knows Dot's no good at things like that, calculating the angles, and furthermore Ralfie would have fallen all over herself if Dot had approached her in those days. She's so insistent that Dot sometimes doubts her own memory. She's right, though.

Their real meeting, the significant one, came later. It was at a dinner party, the usual potluck sort of thing. Ralfie had contributed a liter of Diet Coke, and Dot her one specialty, a rice, black bean, and cheese casserole, the secret ingredient an inordinate amount of cheese. Neither Dot nor Ralfie can remember anymore whom the hostess was, only that Dot had found herself sitting next to an old rival, someone she had once thought would be her enemy forever, because the woman had cut in on Dot's relationship and spirited away her girlfriend, and then Dot had pined after her for so long that based on the experience, she had devised a formula: in a relationship of less than a year, if the length of the relationship equals x, then the time it takes to recover from it equals $2x$, or even $3x$, if you've got it really bad. By the evening of the dinner party, though, all that was in the past, so much so that when Dot first saw her rival, there had been a strange, mistakenly friendly moment when she had sensed they were related but couldn't remember exactly how.

So she turned to the person on her other side, something she wouldn't normally have done except for the awkwardness on her right, because she could never figure out how to start a conversation with a stranger. And that person was Ralfie, transformed. For one thing, she had cut her hair. On the night of Dot's pool debacle, Ralfie had been wearing it in a shoulder-length bob, expertly cut but somehow looking like a wig. Now she had mowed it off—a do-it-yourself, bathroom-mirror job, it looked like—cowlicks sticking up on top and a skinny braid down her back. She had on baggy jeans held up by a heavy leather belt around her narrow hips, and a faded T-shirt that seemed to read, "Stick your finger in a dyke"—although who would wear such a thing? Who would manufacture it? Through the thin cotton of the shirt, Dot could make out Ralfie's nipples and the shape of her breasts—kind of long and saggy. Not the beautiful kind.

"Still playing pool?" Dot asked, bringing up the only thing she knew about the woman.

"Uh-uh. Quit while I was ahead," explained Ralfie, somewhat enigmatically.

"I almost didn't recognize you."

Ralfie nodded. "A lot of people say that. I take it as a compliment."

"I don't know if I meant it one way or the other—"

"Aw, come on. Just say you did." And Ralfie winked at her, a gesture so corny Dot had to admire it, she didn't know anyone else who would have dared. She winked back.

"Hey, got something in your eye?" Ralfie dipped a corner of her napkin in her water glass, reached out, and dabbed at Dot's eyelid.

Dot pushed her hand away. "Of course I don't."

"You were squinting." Suavely, Ralfie winked again. "Let's blow this pop stand." She stood and announced, "So sorry, ladies, I just remembered, my nonna's sick. My grandma, you know. Gotta run."

Expressions of puzzled sympathy from around the table. "Wow, I hope she's okay." "Oh, Ralfie, you should've said something!"

She grabbed Dot's hand and pulled her along. "Yeah, well, thanks. Catch you later." Helped her down the icy front steps. "These girls never shovel their walk. Why is that?"

"I don't know, it doesn't seem very practical, or considerate, really, if you're going to invite people—"

Ralfie waved away her answer. "So, who are you, anyway?"

Dot stared at her. What to say? And really, who was she?

Ralfie laughed. "Don't go all philosophical, it's just a question. You didn't want to stay, did you? I could tell the night was going in the wrong direction. Like that chick on the other side of you? Total home wrecker."

"No kidding," said Dot. Discovering there was a reputation involved was affirming, in a way. It made her feel less of a fool for love.

"But you—why haven't I seen you before?"

Another unanswerable question. Ralfie drove them to her place. "It's small but it's home," she told Dot. "You'll see." She pulled over to get them a pizza, and sitting at the kitchen table, they ate a few slices right out of the box. As ravenous as they were, though, they didn't linger—partly because they knew there was something better just ahead, and partly because the heat in the apartment took its sweet time coming up, and each of them in turn had looked longingly through the door to the next room, at the puffy duvet on the bed. Only after they had crawled under it did they fling off one piece of clothing after another, laughing. "Come closer. Closer. I'm freezing!" It was a reversal of the usual order of things, and it lacked romance—but there would be a long future in warmer rooms to look one another over slowly, to touch, kiss, become acquainted; they could predict that already. Afterward Ralfie rolled on top of Dot, so Dot put her arms around her, and entwined and sweaty, she murmured in Ralfie's ear, "But you have."

"What?"

"Seen me before."

"No way!" said Ralfie.

Dot had been in her last semester of library school then, and Ralfie was already with the DPW, Dot remembers, picturing Ralfie's haircut. The elf-lock hadn't disappeared until a morning in the mid-'90s when, Ralfie offering no explanation, Dot had noticed the long braid in the bathroom trash.

The casserole became a joke between them. Dot never got her pan back.

8

Ralfie on the Job

Ralfie's graduated to a cane, and to her great relief and that of everyone who's had to deal with her, she's back on the job.

"Take it easy," Dot calls after her, on her way out the door. "Remember, Shelly said—"

"Sure, baby," Ralfie calls back. "No worries." *As if,* she thinks. She can hear the guys now, all lisps and falsettos: *Ooo, help girly climb into the big truck.*

They welcome her back, though, presenting her with a drippy cup of coffee—heavy on the cream, three sugars, her usual—and a doughnut, raspberry jelly, the best. Ralfie likes working the early shift, when the buses have just started running and the occasional car speeding by has its headlights on, and the city is hers—she knows its most intimate parts, the pipes below the pavement that keep the whole thing pumping along; the cables twisting and crossing above it, so familiar that most people simply don't see them and believe their view of the sky is unimpeded. That is, until the pipes burst, the wires come down in a storm, and Ralfie and the crew load up the truck bed with a jackhammer or maneuver the cherry picker out of the garage, and they all rack up overtime getting hoisted into the treetops or crawling into manholes. Ralfie dislikes the word *manhole*, but she can't think of an alternative. Dot did a little research project for her in the library, to find a gender-neutral substitute, but *utility access tunnel* is just no fun. So Ralfie will yell, "Whose turn is it to go down this *ass*—I mean, *man*—hole!" It's amazing, actually, that the guys bought her a doughnut.

And with Ralfie back at work, here's another thing about Dot. Throughout all the years of her relationship with Ralfie, Dot's been having an affair. Sort of. She doesn't like to think of it that way, because it sounds so sleazy and deceptive, but what else would you call it? Viola Cottage was her advisor in library school. Which might sound boring: a lady librarian with her glasses on a string around her neck, speaking in whispers and shushing everybody.

But that's not Viola. She was glamorous, or at least Dot thought so—Viola, with her hennaed curls and scarves and beads and eccentric pants. She never went in for the black that Dot affected at the time. She was all color, and Dot found herself wanting that brightness in her life. Religiously she attended Viola's office hours, and when they were no longer advisor and advisee, she invited Viola out for drinks, to celebrate their change of status. A bottle of wine, an unexpected spark, and for a while it was superhot, Dot sneaking around and making excuses to Ralfie about overtime, breakfast meetings, a high school friend in from out of town. They had been living together for only a year or so then, and although they assumed they were monogamous, Dot rationalized to herself that they had never explicitly said so. She wasn't going to be the one to bring it up.

She dared to fabricate a conference. Oh, you know, she told Ralfie. Librarians. Tedious. Sigh. Ralfie didn't ask any questions, didn't seem interested, and Dot and Viola secluded themselves in a New Hampshire motel for an entire weekend. But that did it. The guilt, and also, Dot realized, she craved Ralfie's energy and orneriness. Viola's gentility and intellect—the very things that had drawn Dot to her in the first place—ultimately didn't compare. So then she was making excuses to Viola, who got it right away and steered them toward a friendship—one in which, from time to time, they found themselves physically entangled. Benefiting, as they say. To this day, Dot's never admitted to Ralfie about the benefits, and she represses her regular, guilty urges to cancel her dates.

Lately, though, Viola has lost a bit of her charisma. She takes Dot's arm if they have to walk more than a few paces from the car to Viola's favorite Indian place, and Dot feels the pressure of her hand when they step down a curb or over a frost heave in the sidewalk. "A touch of arthritis," says Viola when she sees Dot's concerned look. "Our evolutionary penalty for standing up from all fours, I suppose."

"So I have that to look forward to?" says Dot.

"Fasten your seatbelt!" says Viola. "As Bette Davis used to say."

"*All about Eve*," says Dot.

Viola gives her bicep another squeeze. "That's why I love you. Do you know, some of the children I meet these days have never been inside a theater? They watch everything on their screens."

"Bette also said, 'Old age ain't for sissies.'"

But at this, Viola glares at her. "Everybody quotes that. I'm beginning to think it's simply homophobic. In this day and age, I'm grateful when our sissies make it into old age. Anyway, I'm not *old* old."

"Eighty? That's not old? I mean, I'm not criticizing. But everyone naturally slows down, don't you think?"

"The new fifty," says Viola. "You'll see. You'll be there yourself soon enough."

But Dot's still trying to figure out—she has been for almost a decade by now—how she could have gotten to sixty. Then to sixty plus. And sixty plus-plus. Like, she was forty, and then suddenly, it was her sixtieth birthday, and Ralfie wanted to throw her a big party. Dot had put her foot down. "That's what *you* want. Not me." They had an expensive, quiet dinner out, and then, when Ralfie's big birthday came around a few months later, they went on a gay cruise. Ralfie ate it up, all of it—the food, the drink, the lesbian comedians, the romantic dress-up evenings. She's been clamoring ever since to go again, and in fact, Dot didn't hate it. The activities were more fun than she would have thought, and she genuinely liked some of the women they met, although they never saw them again after the ship docked, even those they had vowed to keep in touch with. But it was all too . . . too coupled and group-y. All us girls together. When Dot travels, she likes to really see a place, to wander its narrow streets, visit the town museum, with its vitrines displaying donated flotsam from the locals' attics. Shop for groceries, even. On the ship she had had a low, throbbing headache for the entire week.

And now look at her. Sixty-eight, somehow, although she's stopped admitting that to just anyone. She shaves off a year or two, especially when the conversation turns, as it so often does these days, to retirement. She has no intention of going that route, although she supposes she'll have to, some day. But right now, she likes her job, and she and Ralfie are socking away what they can from their paychecks—for when they get, you know, old. To Viola, she concedes, "I guess so. I can feel it coming, some mornings." When she gets out of bed, her hamstrings start in with a peculiar, electrical ache, which is very uncomfortable, like the high pitch of a dental drill, transposed into the muscle.

Viola pats her hand. "You'll be fine. Like me—a tough old bird."

And really, Viola's becoming birdlike, with her inquisitive nose, her clawing hands, her body shrinking and bending down to its essence. Dot does not want to become a bird. In her case she would be a stork or a flamingo, some kind of preposterous, towering species. Viola keeps herself up, dying her curls and, as reading becomes a chore, correcting her vision with outsized, red-framed glasses. She's always trailing a scarf or shawl, in jewel colors—purple, emerald, tangerine—and soft fabrics: chenille, silk, cashmere.

"I'm going to leave these to you," says Viola, fingering today's shawl. "My blankies. You could use a little elegance and comfort in your life, after . . ." She stops herself.

Dot laughs. "I can guess! You almost said, 'after all this time with that prickly Ralfie.' Am I right?"

"Absolutely not!" claims Viola. "That would be very rude. I try never to criticize people's love choices. Who can see into the human heart?"

But Dot notices that Viola doesn't tell her what she was going to say instead. "Whatever you think I need, Vi, Ralfie keeps me on my toes." Feeling strangely breathless, she changes the subject. "Let's order. I'm hungry."

Viola waves her hand in the air, and a waiter comes to stand over their table. "To start I'd like a mango lassi, please," she says. "Not too sweet, if you can manage it. And for lunch we'll share a saag paneer and a bread. A poori, I think."

"Just water to drink for me," says Dot. "And can we have the brown rice instead of white?"

The waiter stares at them, like he can't figure out why these white women are sitting at his table and barking orders at him. He turns and walks away.

"He'll be back," Viola tells Dot. "We've had him before. I don't know why you never see a waitress in this place, I'm sure they'd be more efficient. And wouldn't you love to wear a beautiful sari all the time? I had a colleague, Meena, at the main branch—"

"Not me," says Dot. "I don't think I could manage it."

"Ha!" laughs Viola. "Maybe not. You know, if you don't wrap it correctly, the sari can just fall off! Six yards of material, or whatever it is, in a heap on the floor! That's what Meena told me, although of course hers were perfect. Lovely silks."

A different waiter brings their food. "Chicken spinach," he explains, pointing at each dish. "Paratha bread. Rice to share."

"Oh dear," says Viola. "We wanted the paneer—the cheese—not the chicken, you know. And a poori."

"But this will be fine," Dot says quickly, seeing the waiter's pained look.

He puts the lassi down in front of her. "Mango drink," he says. Dot pushes it across the table to Viola.

"Oh, okay," says Viola. When he leaves, she reaches for the lassi, takes a sip, and shudders. "Sweet," she says. "This always happens here, doesn't it?"

Dot nods. "At least he got the rice right."

"Well, it keeps life interesting—never knowing what you'll get. Although at some point I suppose we should do something about it. May I serve you, darling Dotty?"

Dot looks at her. Viola usually starts with the possessives and the diminutives as a prelude to bed. And indeed, when they've finished their lunch, she says, "Come home with me, sweetness. It's been a long time."

The strange breathlessness catches her again, and Dot says, "I don't think so. Not today." Viola looks at her, surprised, and Dot wonders, has she ever before said no? She feels like a churl. A codpiece. Something medieval. Because frankly, she doesn't want to take on caring for Viola, on top of Ralfie. On top of appeasing Susan. On top of—oh, everything. All she ever does, she thinks, is try to make other people feel good, and suddenly, she's tired. She knows she's just feeling sorry for herself, but if she goes home with Viola, she'll have to give her an arm as they walk to the car, and then, in Viola's bedroom, help her with her buttons. She looks at Viola's hands on the table between them, her swollen knuckles. She doesn't want to help her with her buttons. "I mean, sure," says Dot. "Let's." She'll undo the buttons slow and sexy, she plans, so Viola doesn't see it as helpful.

Viola smiles at her. "Dear heart," she says. "I'll get the check." She stands, leaning on the table, and Dot grabs her shawl as it slides to the floor.

In Viola's bedroom, Dot does her button thing. She reaches around Viola in a hug to undo the hooks on her bra, too, and Viola gives a little shake of her shoulders to make it fall off, revealing her small breasts. They are lovely still; they haven't changed. *Okay, let's do this*, Dot thinks wearily, and she leans down to kiss Viola's nipples, then pauses to make her a nest among the pillows and coverlets. Pulling off the rest of their clothing, they climb in, and Dot resumes kissing Viola's nipples, reaches down to stroke the insides of her thighs, with their soft, loose skin. As long as Dot's known her, the color of the hair on Viola's head, which she hennas to near purple, has never matched that of her pubic hair, now thinning and gray. Dot rests her hand on it for a moment, tries slipping in a finger, pulls it out.

"Suck this," she orders, putting two fingers in Viola's mouth.

"Oh, yes," says Viola cheerfully. "Tell me what to do."

Dot slips her fingers back between Viola's labia, and Viola pulls her close, kisses her deeply, then more distractedly. She turns her head away, arches her back, tightens her hold on Dot. Gasps. "How I missed you, lovely Dot," she says, relaxing and opening her eyes, pulling Dot toward her and giving her a sloppy kiss. "We should do this more often."

"Turn around, baby. Let me hold you from behind," says Dot.

Viola turns, sighs as Dot cups her buttock, and looks over her shoulder. "Now you," she says.

"I'm fine."

"Aww, I want you to come too."

"No, really," says Dot. She does not want to come; it's exhausting. She had figured that once Viola came, she would leave Dot alone. Dot pulls Viola closer and murmurs into the back of her neck, "Just lie still with me, baby. Like this."

Viola flips around and sits up. "What were you doing?" she demands.

"Huh?"

"What were you doing?" she repeats. "Were you doing me a favor?"

"What? But—no! Of course not. Viola!" Dot pleads, because Viola's exactly right. "Lie down, honey."

"Never, ever do that to me again," says Viola. "Not ever. Do not do me any favors."

"Okay, I'm sorry, but you're wrong," Dot lies. "Whatever you're thinking."

Viola stands up from the bed and gathers her clothes from the floor. She sits back down and pulls on her underpants, easily hooks her bra behind her. She looks down at Dot. "So, is that it, then?"

"No," says Dot, propping herself up on her elbow. Although she realizes this probably is. It. Although they'll remain friends.

9

The Weight Slams Down

Dot's first thought, when she feels the weight slam down on her chest and the burning sensation in the back of her throat, is that the disastrous afternoon with Viola wasn't the first time she had felt that breathlessness and exhaustion. It had happened before, late afternoons, driving home from work—a weight on her chest. But it had dissipated. Now she can't get out of bed. She yells for Ralfie, but apparently she doesn't make a sound, because she can hear Ralfie puttering away in the kitchen as time expands, and she must tell someone, tell the world of her discovery, that even now the effects of the primal Big Bang can be felt, even by everyday humans: the universe rushing vertiginously outward and outward, and gravity flattening her to the bed, and oh so many things are being revealed—even though only seconds, by the clock on the bedside table, have passed. And it's as though she can see Ralfie through the wall, the familiar succession of pings and clatter are clearly her, making their morning coffee. Dot tries again to cry out, and this time Ralfie must have heard her squeaking, because she comes limping as fast as she can into the bedroom, calling, "What? What?"

Dot is choking and thrashing around on the bed. "Oh, Jesus, Jesus," says Ralfie. "Lie still, baby. I'm calling an ambulance."

Dot stills. Chokes out, "No, no, I'm okay."

"Not," says Ralfie, pulling her phone out of the holster on her belt and punching in the number.

"I'm scared," whispers Dot.

So Ralfie climbs into the bed with her, boots and all, and she and Dot hold hands until they hear the sirens. "I'm going to get the door," says Ralfie. "Stay right here. You're going to be all right." But *Jesus, Jesus, Jesus*, is all she can think, and she honestly doesn't know if Dot will be all right at all.

"The stairs," says Dot.

Miraculously, Ralfie's limp is gone, and she flies down the stairs like a kid and yanks open the front door. "Up here!" she calls out to the EMTs emerging from the ambulance, and as she yells, "Third floor!" they charge past her, and the weakness in her leg returns, and she collapses onto the bottom step. So she doesn't know what all they have done to Dot when they come charging back down with her on a stretcher, and Ralfie manages to scoot over on the stair to avoid tripping them. As they're sliding Dot into the back of the ambulance, one of them breaks away and jogs back to Ralfie, gives her a hand to help her back to her feet. He glances at her knee brace and the DPW insignia on her shirt. "Adrenaline," he says. "Amazing shit, right? Your lady's asking for you, dude, and I'd let you in the back of the vehicle, but we've got to get her hooked up, you know?"

"I'll stay out of the way," says Ralfie.

"Sorry, no can do. You can drive, right? With the knee?"

"Sure, whadda you think?" says Ralfie, annoyed to be caught out in her weakness. But the guy's a pro, he's got her figured out.

"Meet us at the ER."

Somehow she's handling the car like a race driver, screeching around the turns, and her thought processes are rushing forward too, crystal clear. Adrenaline.

She and Dot never considered this, she realizes—that they both could be laid up at the same time. Somehow, during all the years of their relationship, it's never happened. Or if it has, it's been simultaneous colds, nothing serious, and they would spend a pleasant day or two on the couch, one at each end, blowing their noses and napping and listening to Ralfie's collection of albums and old 45s, which even back in high school she had insisted on keeping in pristine shape, letting no one else touch them, so they're mostly still playable. She and Dot would bicker about whose turn it was to get up and flip them over; the B-sides are full of surprises. Aretha, Curtis Mayfield, the Shirelles, Johnny Mathis—whom Dot can't stand, that sentimental catch in his voice, so they would bicker about him, too. They haven't done any of that in ages, though, and Ralfie smiles as she imagines digging out her records as a surprise for Dot, when she comes home. *Meet the Beatles.* She hums, *Yeah, yeah, yeah.*

Ralfie snaps to. It's weird, how even in an emergency the mind drifts into irrelevance. Self-protection, she guesses. Dot will come home, and

Ralfie will set her up to recuperate on the couch. Dot will come home. She will recuperate. Ralfie pushes other thoughts out of her head.

Except that Ralfie too still needs her time on the couch, leg iced and elevated. So then who will bring them things? Shelly? The girl only ever came for a couple of hours a week, and since Ralfie's gotten more mobile, she doesn't come at all. It's not her job, anyway.

Best case, Ralfie tries to imagine, to encourage herself, *What?* She can't come up with anything.

I O

Oxygen

In Cardio Care, Dot's on oxygen, tubes up her nose. Her nightie has been replaced with a hospital gown. She didn't exactly pass out at home, but somehow she can't recall all the steps of how she ended up here. She keeps trying to put them in order in her mind but ends up every time with a horrible jumble of lights and noise and being tossed around and palpated and jabbed. There's an IV in her arm and wires pasted all over her chest. She's exhausted and wants to sleep, but when she closes her eyes, there's the jumble again, the lights, noise, palpating, etcetera. They've positioned her on the bed with the monitors behind her, so she has no idea what her vital signs are. If she has any. A machine starts beeping, and she can't discern whether it's in her cubicle or the one next to her until a nurse rushes in, taps the IV, pushes a button on a machine, checks the monitors. "Don't worry, dear, you're fine," she says, rushing out again.

Not reassuring, Dot thinks. In the ambulance, they gave her a teeny pink cube of a baby aspirin to chew, and that wasn't reassuring either. At least they could have dosed her with a big-girl aspirin. And who knows what they're dripping into her now. The pain in her chest has receded, mostly, and she would be feeling almost normal, except for the exhaustion. The hospital, she had noticed back when Ralfie had her knee surgery, automatically makes even the healthiest specimen feel just this side of dead. Ralfie had turned pale as soon as she and Dot had crossed the lobby threshold, before she had been prepped or anything. Now, in this room, no one's explaining anything, which is, Dot thinks, just plain mean. And where is Ralfie?

Ralfie's here. She throws herself onto Dot and covers her face with kisses, and all the machines start beeping at once, at different pitches, unsynchronized. "Oh, my Dotty, my Dotty!" is all Ralfie can say. "Jesus, Mary, and Joseph."

The nurse rushes back in. "What's going on in here?" she yells at Ralfie. "What have you done?" She pushes some buttons until the noises stop, untangles and resticks the wires on Dot's chest, examines the bag on the IV pole, frowns. "Be gentle, can't you? And get off her bed. She's going to be fine."

"Right," says Ralfie, standing up. She points at the machines. "Then what's all this for?"

The nurse doesn't answer, turns and leaves.

Ralfie to the rescue. Dot giggles. "Don't alienate her, honey. She's gotta take care of me."

Ralfie stares at her. "What's so funny? What are they putting in that IV, anyway? Has the doc been here?"

"I'm not sure," says Dot. "Which one is the doctor? So many people, in and out. It's confusing."

"Confusing." Ralfie shakes her head. "I'm going to find somebody who knows what's what."

"No, stay with me."

Ralfie sits carefully back on the bed, takes Dot's hand. "I'm right here."

"Someone will come soon. They can't stand to leave me alone, you'll see."

Ralfie looks around. "I wish I could take you home. You know. Blow this pop stand."

"Yeah, blow it," Dot repeats. So now she is reassuring Ralfie, and shouldn't it be the other way around? Everything in this hospital is upside down and backward.

"This sucks," Ralfie declares, as a wedge formation of doctors and interns bursts into the room and circles around her bed.

"No big hurry or nothing," Ralfie says to them. "It's just my wife having a heart attack."

The doctor turns to his students. "The sense of time is distorted," he points out. To Ralfie, he says, "She is getting the best care. You can stay while we examine her, but please stand over there, out of the way." As he assesses the monitors, a student lifts Dot's arm to check her pulse, and another takes her chart from the foot of the bed and flips through it. Another feels her ankles. "No swelling," she calls.

"Very good," says the doctor. "You see, guys, even with all this"—he gestures toward the monitors—"the physician's touch is often the most sensitive instrument." He puts a stethoscope to Dot's chest, and the rest of them crowd around to watch. Finally the doctor looks up, addresses Dot. "You'll have to stay with us for a day or two, Ms. Greenbaum, until we can make sure you're stable. But I believe you will make a full recovery. Good as new, you know."

From her corner, Ralfie glares at the medical students. "Write that down. All the big docs say it. 'Good as new.'"

The doctor and his students ignore her. "A couple month's rest and then a few lifestyle changes, gentle exercise, attention to diet, a daily aspirin. Rest," he emphasizes. "You don't have a history of clotting disorders, do you?"

Dot shakes her head.

"Of course not!" calls Ralfie.

"No, of course not," says the doctor. "You've been quite healthy. Until this little episode. Okay, guys, let's get a move on. Thank you, Ms. Greenbaum." He shakes Dot's hand and turns to Ralfie. "Thanks, pal." And repeats, almost to himself, "Good as new."

The students smile at this positive prognosis and one by one shake Dot's hand and file out.

Ralfie hobbles back to the bed and sits down heavily.

"Knee hurt?" asks Dot.

"Just tired." She takes Dot's hand again. Anger and attitude gone for once, she looks at Dot. "What are we going to do?"

Dot looks back at her. "I don't know." Does "rest" mean "sick leave"? The children are always giving her their colds and viruses, which can't be good, in her condition. Whatever that is. But she's pretty sure her insurance doesn't cover disability. And what about when Ralfie has the other knee done? How will they pay the mortgage? It's not huge, at this point, but it exists, and then there's the cable bill, which is insanely high, between Ralfie's sports stations and Dot's movies—and she's not going to cancel it now, not if they're going to be at home "resting" all the time. Food. Taxes. It's too much to think about, and she shuts her eyes. "One thing at a time," she tells Ralfie, whom she can feel hovering over her. "First I've got to get out of here."

We gotta get out of this place, Ralfie hums, a tune from one of the old 45s. *If it's the last thing we ever do.*

I I

All Sorts of New Vocabulary

Dot and Ralfie learn all sorts of new vocabulary: angioplasty, aorta, thrombosis. "In my day, they just called it a coronary," says Ralfie. "It took out the old *zios*. Them and their cigars."

"We know more now," says the cardiologist. "We've made a lot of progress. Stenting was a fantastic advance. Most patients can go home the next day."

"Amazing," says Dot, trying to hear this as good news. Stent: noun. To stent: verb.

"Yes, and you'll be awake during the whole procedure."

"What?" says Dot. "That's awful! I don't want to feel you cutting me! Can't I be put to sleep?"

"I'm afraid not, Ms. Greenbaum. We may need to ask you questions or give you instructions. But you'll have a local anesthetic. And our man is excellent. You won't feel anything. The incisions are minimal."

Anesthetic. Incisions. More words. How people get through this horror Dot can't imagine, but then she does, somehow—what choice does she have?—and just as the doctor said, she's released from the hospital. Or rather, she's kicked out, since she could really have used a little more time to recuperate—but that's the way things work these days. Iatrogenic. Another word: an illness caused by the treatment itself. Hang out in the hospital longer than a couple of days, and you risk a flesh-eating staph infection or something equally life threatening and disgusting.

Dot's body has betrayed her in such an unexpected and uncalled-for way, and then has endured so many assaults from the outside, that Dot hardly knows who she is anymore, or what it is to feel normal. She can't remember normal, just the hospital bed, and every time she wakes, a new ache or stabbing pain, or an apparently adolescent nurse taking her blood pressure.

How she and Ralfie, neither of them medically trained, will manage her care, Dot can't imagine. She's read the pages of instructions they've given her—wound care, medication schedules, warning signs. A phone number to call in case of emergency. In case this chronic emergency she's in becomes acute. It's overwhelming, far more than two laypeople—one of them the patient, one of them Ralfie—should be expected to handle. But the next thing Dot knows, she's being discharged with a fistful of orange pill bottles, an orderly pushing her in a wheelchair and a nurse walking alongside. The orderly maneuvers her through the revolving door at the hospital entrance—and there's Ralfie. "Thank god," says Dot.

"You can walk from here," the nurse tells Dot. "The chair is just our procedure."

So Dot gets to her feet, feeling a little wobbly, and falls into Ralfie's arms.

"You're coming home!" says Ralfie. "I missed you so much, baby."

"Oh, me too," says Dot, trying to match Ralfie's emotion, although she's feeling strangely blank inside. What will home be like, now that she is so changed? "But you were here every day. How could you miss me?"

"I just could! At night. In our bed."

"Me too," Dot repeats. When they get to their building, she has to literally drag herself up the stairs to the apartment, hand over hand on the banister, Ralfie following, to catch her if she topples, although Ralfie herself is leaning on her cane with one hand, and with the other carrying a plastic bag from the hospital containing Dot's few possessions: her nightie, her watch, a stack of get-well cards, a mystery featuring a female detective— a gift from Viola that she hadn't been able to muster the concentration to read. Every time she opened the book, the detective was stuck in traffic.

"All I want to do is sleep," Dot says as they walk in the door. And she proceeds to do almost nothing but, and in the bed, not on the couch, where she and Ralfie nap. Dot's sleeping is not napping. It's deep, intermittently troubled by nightmares of suffocation.

12

Ralfie Feels Desperate

Ralfie feels so desperate she calls Susan.

"I had no idea you had my number," says the surprised Susan.

"Well, I do," says Ralfie. "I just never used it. But I've got to talk to some-body who knows Dot. She's not herself, you know? I mean, have you noticed?"

"She's been home for what? A couple of weeks? What do you expect her to be like? Even I'm still in shock—Dot having a heart attack. Dot, of all people! I would have thought it would be you, if anybody—"

"Gee, thanks," says Ralfie, trying to ignore any implications. It's just Susan's way.

"Well, I'm sorry, but my sister's just had major surgery. I'm upset. And of course she's tired."

"No, it's not that. It's something about her, her—"

"I have noticed," Susan admits. "Give her some time."

"It's been a month."

"Two weeks," Susan repeats. "Do you always have to exaggerate?"

"Uh-huh," says Ralfie, who can't resist needling her, even now, while asking for her help. "Anyway, it's not an exaggeration. It *feels* like a month."

"People get depressed. You can understand that, can't you?"

"Some people," says Ralfie. "Not my Dot."

Susan sighs. "I'll be over this evening."

"Thanks," says Ralfie, meaning it. It's hard for her to get the words out, but she manages, growling in her Mr. Belrose voice, "Appreciate it."

Susan arrives with a bag full of take-out containers and starts distribut-ing paper plates and napkins around the table. "Sit, sit!" she tells Dot and Ralfie. "I stopped at Whole Foods."

Ralfie groans.

"What?" says Susan. "Their prepared foods always look so good, I've wanted to try them. And this is no time for pizza, because Dot, you know—"

"I'm fine," Dot cuts her off. "Pizza would've been fine. I can eat whatever—"

"I don't think so," says Susan, opening containers. "This is garden salad, and here's some brown rice, and this one is tofu—"

"I knew it!" says Ralfie. "Whole so-called Foods. I can't eat that tofu stuff, it doesn't have any taste, and it feels creepy when you try to chew it."

"So actually, you're afraid of tofu," says Susan.

"Yup," says Ralfie.

"I got some chicken cutlets, you can eat those," says Susan.

"Just a small piece of chicken for me," says Dot.

Susan makes up a plate for her with salad and rice and chicken and a slab of tofu.

"Susan," says Dot. "You are sweet to bring us dinner, but I can't eat all that. I don't have much of an appetite—"

"Just try it," says Susan. "It's good for you." She turns to Ralfie. "You too." She makes herself a generous plate, like the one she served Dot, while Ralfie and Dot, each for her own reasons, pick at their dinners. "I wish you guys would reconsider about Maple Grove," she says suddenly.

"Give it up, Susan." Dot sighs. "You're making me feel worse. Anyway, how could we manage moving, right now?"

Dot's pill bottles clutter the kitchen counter. Ralfie has folded her heirloom afghan—her nonna's handiwork, in the colors of the Italian flag—invitingly on the couch, where she wishes Dot would plant herself. So far, though, Dot's shut herself in the bedroom, and it's Ralfie who wraps the afghan around her shoulders every evening and by herself watches whatever sport shows up on TV. Football, golf, tennis. Bicycle racing—which is exceptionally boring, the competitors' lycraed butts bobbing across the screen. One time she dozed off and swears she woke to see people jousting—but Dot says she must have dreamed that. Ralfie says she saw what she saw.

"Dot's right," says Ralfie. "Quit trying to pack us off to the old-age home."

"For the millionth time, it's *not*—"

"Yeah, it is," says Ralfie.

"You know," says Susan, "all day people come to me for advice. I have good ideas! The only ones who don't think so are you two. My own family!"

"Oh, come on, we listen to you a lot," Dot tries to placate her. "But this time—"

"Germaine and I went back to see that condo again. We're seriously thinking of making an offer."

Dot and Ralfie stare at Susan, silenced.

"You're kidding," says Ralfie. "Maple Grave?"

"But you always say you love your place," says Dot.

"I haven't said that for a long time," says Susan. "In case you haven't noticed. I'm sick of everything falling apart all the time. I got hit with a big assessment for a new roof last year. Then the water heater went. I've been saving for a down payment. Why do you think I started the coaching business?"

"Water heaters always go," says Ralfie. "They flood and everything in the basement gets all—"

"I'm aware of that, believe me," says Susan. "And from now on somebody else is going to take care of it. And the snow shoveling." She turns to Dot. "Which you, Dorothy, should never do again, in your condition."

"Maple Grave!" Dot shakes her head. "I just can't believe it. You'll be so far away."

"Don't call it that! And I won't be far away. Not if you come too—"

"Of course I'd never let her shovel the walk!" says Ralfie.

"Right. So you'll do it, Miss Gimpy," says Susan.

"Wow," says Ralfie. "I guess you forgot what I do all day. On the truck."

"Susan," says Dot. "Please." Actually, Dot doubts that Ralfie's touched a shovel since she's been back on the job. The guys watch out for her. "I never expected this. I don't think I can take it in." She stands up. "I'm going inside."

"Look what you've done!" Ralfie hisses at Susan. "Some help you are!"

"Just be realistic for once," Susan hisses back. "Elevator, parking, that concierge taking care of any problems. If we all moved up there together, you wouldn't have to worry about Mr. Belrose."

"Sounds great," says Ralfie. "A bunch of decrepit old lesbians. I can just picture us in our rocking chairs." She stands to clear the table.

"I'll do that," says Susan, so Ralfie sits back down, and Susan bustles around, gathering up the paper plates and napkins and stuffing them in the trash, wrapping the leftovers. "There. All done."

"You can take those with you," says Ralfie.

"Gee thanks," says Susan. "I think I will. I'll have a good lunch." She wets a sponge, gives the table a few swipes.

"Dot's not going to come out of there for the rest of the night, you know," says Ralfie. "This is just what I was talking about."

"You asked me to help, remember? No wonder she's depressed, you two are in a rut in this place."

After Susan leaves, Ralfie goes into the bedroom and lies down next to Dot, but Dot rolls away from her. Ralfie taps her on the shoulder. "Guess what?" she says, attempting cheer. "Tofu for breakfast."

Dot squeezes her eyes shut, pretends to sleep. Why Susan's become so obsessed with the horrible Maple Grave is beyond her. After they visited the place, Dot thought they all felt basically the same way: it was a joke. An amusing way to spend a morning. Mr. Belrose. What she can't figure out is, if Susan's so crazy about Germaine, why would she want to drag her way out there, where Germaine would be the youngest person for miles? More mysteriously, why would Germaine agree to it? But has she? And now Susan wants Dot and Ralfie to go too? It's all a perverse expression of Susan's need for approval. She's uncomfortable until everyone else likes and wants the same things she does. Maybe she's gotten worse lately. Maybe they've all gotten worse, Dot thinks, and with that, suddenly falls asleep.

Ralfie lies awake beside her, staring at the ceiling, her non-bionic knee throbbing.

13

The Characteristic Housing

The characteristic housing of formerly industrial Massachusetts cities and towns is the triple-decker. In Worcester, in Pittsfield, in New Bedford and Boston's outlying neighborhoods, they're all you see, block after block of wood-frame, bay-windowed, flat-roofed boxes—three-flats, six-flats. Some with back porches, although those tend to fall down over the years. Working-class housing. The one Dot and Ralfie live in is about a hundred years old. The sills in the basement, the inspector told them when they bought the third floor, are made from repurposed ships' decking, which Dot has always thought is very romantic but which means, basically, scrap. Back in the day, parents and kids would be jammed into two or three bedrooms in the middle apartment, the in-laws on the floors above and below. These days, the triple-deckers have been condo-ized floor by floor—at least in gentrifying neighborhoods—and the apartments are more typically lived in by singles or couples, who swoon over the built-in china cabinets, the pocket doors, and the moldings—that is, if some misguided landlord hasn't painted them over in an attempt to hide the decades' scars and gouges. Over the years, owners have remodeled—in Dot and Ralfie's condo, the wall between the kitchen and the dining room was taken down, creating a nice open floor plan and breezes in the summer—but the basic layouts of the triple-deckers are all the same. Dot can find the bathroom at the home of anyone she visits.

Since Dot's been recuperating, she and Viola don't go out to lunch; instead Viola comes over for afternoon tea. And lectures. "I don't see why your sister thinks you have to move out to some suburban wasteland. In my opinion, the city is an excellent place for elders. You have public transit, hospitals. And of course all the wonderful cultural opportunities."

"I guess so," says Dot. Is it her imagination, or is everyone trying to tell her what to do these days?

"If only these three-deckers had elevators."

"They don't need them," says Dot, pulling out a bit of wisdom she's learned from Ralfie, who knows all sorts of obscure city ordinances. "They're only required for buildings over three stories."

"Well, that is too bad. Tricky of them." Viola looks at the coffee table in front of them. Their mugs and the plate of stale cookies that Dot put out are empty. Viola presses her index finger into the crumbs, licks it. Innocently, she looks out the window. "What a lovely day!" she exclaims. "A good afternoon for a walk, don't you think?"

"The doctor did say I should walk every day. But I haven't felt up to it.

"You're overthinking. You have to *just do it*, as they say."

"Not today, okay, Vi?" says Dot. "I'll just-do-it soon. But not now."

After Viola leaves, though, Dot finds herself staring into her closet, hoping her sneakers will appear. Viola is right about one thing: Dot hasn't left the house since her last doctor appointment. She finds the sneakers, wraps a scarf around her neck, bundles herself into her coat. Descending the stairs, she clings to the bannister, and on the sidewalk in front of the building, she looks around. The sun is shining, just as Viola pointed out. Dot hears the recorded announcements from the bus stopping on her corner and then the bells from the nearby church counting off the hour. The neighborhood is the same as usual, but somehow it feels different. Her recent lack of familiarity, she supposes. Slowly, she sets off in the wrong direction—not toward the bus stop or the park or the market or any of the places she and Ralfie usually go.

There's a building a few blocks away that she's always tried to ignore. It's so out of scale with the neighborhood that it dwarfs everything in the vicinity, even the sidewalk trees—like it was delivered intact from Manhattan. Dot stops and reads the sign in front of it: "Garden House, Senior Living." The label is entirely aspirational, since it's nothing like a house; it's a brick tower, surrounded by patches of yellowing grass. The garden, Dot supposes. And what kind of living do the seniors here do? But the place surely has an elevator.

For the hell of it, she opens the gate, crosses the grounds, and tries a door marked "Rental Office." A harried-looking woman emerges from behind a tall counter to unlock it. "I guess you're here for the tour," she says.

"Okay," says Dot. "Why not?"

The two of them crowd into a small elevator. It's slow and jerky, and it doesn't seem to have an inspection certificate or an emergency button.

Although Dot is not usually claustrophobic, she begins to wonder how often it breaks down. At least it has no mirror on the wall—for some reason, there's one on the ceiling—and it's not playing music. It deposits them in a long hallway with a linoleum floor. The place is utterly silent, no rustling, no footsteps. Shouldn't there be noises of some sort, Dot wonders, some evidence of human habitation—a TV yakking, a dog barking, a grandchild practicing the piano? There's the same bready smell she remembers from visiting her grandmother, where it wasn't unpleasant, but here it is mixed with disinfectant. The walls are cinderblock.

Her guide offers no information, or even a friendly chat. This tour is perfunctory compared to her visit to Maple Grove. Dot follows her down the hallway, and at one point, her guide unhitches a ring of keys from her belt, flips through it, and unlocks an apartment. She ushers Dot inside. "These tenants are traveling, and they were kind enough to let us show their place to prospective neighbors. They've made it into a real home. I'll let you explore." She waits in the doorway, and Dot wanders around.

The apartment is oddly characterless, even though the residents have cluttered it with family photos and souvenirs of their travels, lumpy pieces of pottery and a model of a red London phone booth, in an attempt to make it more distinctive and personal. The bathroom has a walk-in shower with grab bars, and a white plastic curtain, which depresses her. She imagines mold growing on the bottom of it, even though it is perfectly clean. For now.

Back in the office, the guide's speech is discouraging. She resumes her place behind the counter, asks Dot a few questions about her finances, and scribbles some calculations on a piece of scrap paper. To qualify as low income, Dot and Ralfie would have to make—"Let's see." She looks up at Dot. "Twenty percent of the median income in the city. So that means you could only bring in, say, fifty grand for two. You're married, right?"

"Well, yeah," Dot admits. "But we make more than that. I don't think we could get by if we didn't."

"Exactly. So then you'd have to pay the market rate. Plus an entry fee, of course."

"The market rate around here?" says Dot. "But that would be, what?"

"Depends on the unit," says the guide wearily. "For a two-bedroom? Three to four thousand per month. It includes parking, though," she adds encouragingly.

"That's impossible!" says Dot. "We'd be paying a huge chunk of our income for rent! And then what about when we retire? We have to save."

"Oh, you're retiring? Look, those are the rules. *I* don't make them. *I* can't afford to live here either."

In a way, it's a relief. Elevator or not, Dot can't see her and Ralfie living in a place with a hallway that smells like that. The triple-decker will have to do. It has shipboards! And it's paid for. Almost.

14

A Person of Strong Character

Dot has always thought of herself as a person of strong character. Even as an adolescent, when so many find themselves at sea, pushed back and forth by the daily tides and tumbled in random waves, she knew who she was. She set her course. If certain persistent thoughts and desires meant she was a lezzie homo, then she would *be* a lezzie homo, striding the high school corridors in thick-soled boots so heavy that by the end of the day her calves ached. Growing pains. They went away after a while.

Since her tour of the neighborhood elderly housing, she's decided: she will just have to get better. She's had it with Viola and Susan and even Ralfie telling her what to do and going on about elevators.

Each morning, she waits for Ralfie to leave for work, chokes down a healthful egg-white omelet, and leaves too, for her own work. At first, a walk around the block wears her out, but step by step, she goes a little farther each day, a little faster.

She starts to miss her job. The children.

She didn't at first. She felt so exhausted that she couldn't imagine how she could ever have done it. Couldn't imagine doing it again. Chasing the occasional kindergartner escaping down the hall; bending and reaching to shelve the returns. Really it wasn't all that strenuous, but in those early days, she had been wary of any exertion, no matter how minor. She didn't know what had set off her heart attack—the cardiologist tried to tell her it was not one thing in particular—and she was afraid to trigger it again.

But the children, she realizes, are more dear to her now, in her recovery, than ever: their continual discoveries and their concentration on every little thing. Putting a hand in a pocket. Raising an umbrella. Dot, as an adolescent with dawning self-awareness, had looked back and promised herself she would always remember what it was like—and she does her best.

She used to walk the few blocks to her elementary school—it wasn't unusual in those days for children to wander unaccompanied—and the winding streets were magic: every house, every tree, charged with its own particular character. Its own soul. On some days, she walked carefully, avoiding the sidewalk cracks (*step on a crack, you'll break your mother's back*)—and on others, she jumped methodically from crack to crack. At home she was reprimanded for dawdling yet again. She would note the changing materials of the sidewalks—from concrete slabs to blue-gray slate and back—and examine the dirt nests around the trees, littered with dead leaves and cigarette butts and acorns, or sheets of sycamore bark, its scent earthy and fecal. Even now, Dot dreams, and waking wonders: was there really a store on the corner, across from the house in which her fifth-grade teacher lived—or was that store, in an old, raw-shingled cottage, a figment? What on earth would it have sold?

She especially identifies with the kids who suddenly figure out reading—probably the thing that led her to librarianship in the first place. She remembers the moment in her own life, when the two *o*'s in *look* became first eyes, then letters, and finally, a pronounceable word emerged. It doesn't happen that way for everyone, she's learned; for some it comes piece by piece, and for some the letters swim and swim. But there are always a few like her, and she slips them chapter books.

"Isn't that one for the more advanced learners?" Jim, this year's intern, asked when he caught her at it.

"That kid can handle it," says Dot. "You can't always go by what your professors tell you. You develop an instinct."

One weekend, hiking the path around the local pond with Ralfie, Dot passes the dog walkers, the double strollers, the Russian couples apparently deep in philosophical debate but maybe just arguing about whose turn it is to do the laundry, and outpaces her. Dot's exercise regimen has worked. "I'm going back to work on Monday," she calls back to Ralfie. She stops and waits. "I've used up all my sick time."

"Is that a good idea?" pants Ralfie, hobbling up. Dot's still on more medication than Ralfie can keep track of; she has myriad doctor appointments.

"Who knows what those children have been getting up to without me?" Dot's voice goes shrill as she tries to sound upbeat. "My library is probably complete chaos."

"What about unpaid leave?" Ralfie persists. "We can swing it for another month." The DPW brought in a financial advisor, who gave Ralfie and the guys a few free sessions, and they were told to keep three-months' expenses in their savings. The guys laughed it off—yeah, right, the kids' shoes, the car payments—but Dot and Ralfie took it to heart.

"Rafaella! No. I've never been unpaid in my whole life."

"Whoa, baby," says Ralfie. "Calling me by my full name. This conversation is getting serious."

"Yes, it is! I can't not work. Don't you get it? Otherwise I'll never go out. I'll die."

"What do you mean, die?" says Ralfie, horrified. "You won't die. I won't let you."

"I need to work. Try to understand me for once!"

"Why can't you start slow, a day or two a week?"

"Because I've already spoken to the principal, and she told the substitute not to bother coming in anymore. So," Dot concludes, her jaw clenched, "I am going. Back. To. Work."

When Dot gets like this, Ralfie knows from experience, there's no talking to her. She takes Dot's elbow, and they continue along together, fuming silently at each other. A team of college girls, charmingly multiracial, all of them wearing wool watch caps, and running shorts despite the cold, comes barreling toward them, yelling, "Watch it, watch it!" and forces them off the path.

"Watch it yourself, assholes!" Ralfie yells back, brandishing her cane. It feels great to have someone to shout at and threaten, and she repeats, "Assholes!" But she can tell, as they pass, that the girls are laughing at her.

Dot sighs. It's just so much wasted emotion, as far as she can tell. When they get home, she's planning to dig through her closet to find an outfit for tomorrow that doesn't sag right off her because she's lost too much weight—so say the doctors. She'll prepare a sandwich for her lunch. Count out her pills.

Ralfie interrupts her thoughts, as, Dot's been noticing lately with some annoyance, she so often does. "Hey, listen. Your sister didn't really put a deposit on that place, did she?"

"Susan?" says Dot. "She could've. How would I know?"

"Because she's your sister and you talk, like, every other day?"

"Not these days," Dot admits. Susan is annoyed with her. At first she was all empathy, calming Ralfie, dropping by for visits, bringing Dot tempting little cupcakes and other treats, which Ralfie scarfed down after Susan left.

Dot has never had a sweet tooth, she craves salt, which she's supposed to cut back on, as Susan unfortunately knows. But Dot's lethargy, or whatever it is, discouragement, has crossed some sort of Susan-mandated timeline, and she's taken to plaguing Dot with pep talks. Dot's started to avoid her.

"Could you ask her?"

"I'd rather not," says Dot. "Why do you care?"

"Oh, you know . . ." The truth is, Ralfie, of all people, is starting to think that Susan has a point. There's the other-knee issue, which she's finding herself less and less able to ignore since the first knee was fixed—either in comparison, or because she puts more weight on it, and since it's now the weaker of the two, that hurts, despite the physical therapy and her efforts at exercise. "Just curious."

"You're curious about Susan?" This is so unlikely that Dot understands that Ralfie has an agenda. Fortunately, they're home so she doesn't need to find it out. "I've got my key," she says. "Come on."

Grabbing the shaky stair rail, Ralfie follows Dot up the front steps. She's winded before they reach the second floor; in fact, it takes willpower for her not to grab Dot's arm to steady herself, which is humiliating for a person who once prided herself on her stamina.

Ralfie brings up the question again over dinner. It's her turn to cook, and she wishes Dot would do more than just move the food around on her plate. "Do you think they accepted Susan's offer?"

This time the light dawns. "I am not moving to Maple Grave!" They've used the joke name so often that it's become the only name they use. A sort of dead metaphor. "I thought we agreed on that. We're city people. Susan too, I don't know what's got into her."

"I know, I know. I just . . ." Ralfie hesitates, then confesses in a rush, "I don't think we can keep living here, Dotty. It's too hard, just getting in and out. You said yourself, if you don't go to work, you'll never leave the house."

"That's not what I meant!"

"So your sister's nuts. I've always thought that anyway. But something's got to give, don't you think?"

"No. I don't," cries Dot. Images crowd her head—long, sterile corridors. The feeling of suffocation. "I'm not leaving. You can go where you want, but I'm staying right here." Tears fill her eyes. "We'll split up—is that what you're saying?"

Ralfie stares at her, blind-sided by how quickly things have escalated and the crazy direction they're taking. "But that's not—no!" she stutters. In all these years, they've never had an argument that drew Dot's tears or a threat like this, even the ones that spilled over into the next day—and forget about "don't go to bed angry," they've both had their nights of sleeping on the couch. But those were child's play. This, Ralfie realizes, is the shit.

Dot stands. She stacks their plates, piles them into the sink, and turns the water on to the max so it rushes loudly out of the faucet, muffling conversation. She has nothing more to say, about anything. Ralfie calls out something or other, but Dot turns her back, takes a pot from the stove, scrubs frantically.

Ralfie's just repeating, "Dot! Listen! Dot!" But Dot's not backing down.

15

It Doesn't End There

It doesn't end there. Somehow, they've stopped speaking to each other, except when absolutely necessary. Don't forget to pay the gas bill, that kind of thing. We're out of milk.

Dot herself has to wonder why she's so adamant about not moving. She likes their apartment well enough. Their neighborhood is attractive and convenient—close to a bus stop and a corner store. There's enviable green space: the pond, the big arboretum. Within just a few blocks, you can eat a taco or a plate of biryani; you can get a haircut or buy a hat. The residents are eclectic and tolerant: they pride themselves on their humanistic values, their civic engagement, their support of the arts. They love people of all races, from all parts of the world; some of them post signs in their yards and front windows proclaiming these views. They smile approvingly at Dot and Ralfie, walking down the street holding hands. On weekends they're out and about, taking the kids to the library across the street, walking the dog, putting out the recycling. There's a guy next door who plays the saxophone, blatting away at all hours. Annoying, but also admirable. He never seems to get any better, but he keeps trying.

Still, after all, in Boston, in Cambridge across the river, there are neighborhoods with similar attributes.

But Dot lives in this one. Here, she's handed an apple by a neighbor who just picked it off a tree in their front yard; she spots a quarter on the sidewalk but doesn't stoop to pick it up; overnight, the gingko across the street turns a blinding yellow. There's the corner store, oddly sprawling. It sells quarts of milk, chicken parts, fifty-pound sacks of rice, and off-brand booze. Men lean on the counter, contending in Spanish, but when she holds out her bills, the cashier tears himself away from his buddies and greets her in friendly English. The polite words she practiced—*buenos días, señor, leche por favor, muchas gracias*—flee her mind.

The place is home, simple as that.

When she was coming up in the lesbian community, there was a saying: you can have a great job, a great relationship, or a great place to live, but you can't have all three. She would pointlessly interrogate herself: which would she pick? Not that she had a choice. And maybe the saying was true for people in their twenties, but it no longer applies. In her sixties, Dot has a good life.

The saying had nothing in it about health, or elevators.

Down at the DPW garage, the guys reassure Ralfie. Shawn offers his wisdom. "Aw, she'll come around. Look at me—Clarice says she wouldn't go camping and sleep on the ground if you paid her. So, I take her up on it. I say, 'Okay, baby, I'll pay you. Come with me this weekend and you've got yourself a new wool coat.' 'Coat!' she says. 'You mean for the kids, not me.' 'Fine,' I say. 'Whatever you want.' So we stick the kids with her mom for the weekend, and she comes camping with me, and then last summer we all go, the whole family. I sent away for this pump thing that plugs into the truck dash and blows up a double air mattress, and Clarice, turns out she loves it. She says the hiking's invigorating, and it tires out the kids so they fall asleep as soon as the sun goes down, practically. And we get a little time to ourselves, you know, on the air mattress. Ain't nothing like a little nookie in the great outdoors!"

The guys all laugh and slap Shawn on the back, but his story isn't convincing, and Ralfie can't see what's in it for her. She notes that Clarice is still not sleeping on the ground. And that she never got a coat. Anyway, Clarice is not as demanding as Shawn is always making her out to be; in fact, she's kind of timid, and at parties she and Dot make a point of calling her over. They've never gotten her to talk about anything but her kids, though. Twins, apparently. Shawna and Shavonne. Clarice admits she sometimes wonders if Shawn can tell them apart. She's started putting different color barrettes in their hair—red for Shawna, purple for Shavonne—but he forgets to check. "I know them, of course," she boasts. "I'm their mother."

Neither Ralfie nor Dot has ever been anyone's mother. *No kids* was something they had agreed upon from the start. Which they had had to do, since by the time they got together, it was the start of the lesbian baby boom, when all you needed was a Grey Poupon jar, a cooperative male, a porno mag, and a syringe. As soon as your friends realized you were a serious couple, they wanted to know when you were having children, and how—adoption, AI, or even a bout of old-fashioned sexual intercourse with an unsuspecting former boyfriend. It seemed like half the community was popping out pregnant, and in the lesbian bars they would all be standing around drinking club soda and stroking their bellies—which was maybe why the bars started shutting down right around then, although even before all the club soda, the bartenders used to complain that the lesbians didn't drink enough and on top of that were deadbeat tippers. And then, with all those babies, who had time anymore for dancing and singing? So these days you're lucky to find a once-a-month ladies' night in a back room somewhere.

Maybe, Ralfie thinks, they should have planned things differently and not been so adamant about the kid thing. Shawn and Clarice have their red-headed brats to minister to them in their old age, while who do she and Dot have? Not that Ralfie would want to saddle any child of hers with herself, a lame old geezer who will probably go deaf and demented to boot; it runs in the family. Well before the end, her dear old nonna had stopped listening to her, and in her final year had become convinced that Ralfie was someone named Gino Peruzzi, whom no one could identify. But he was not someone Nonna had been fond of.

Ralfie tries to think—do she and Dot know any young people? They should befriend some, she decides. Muscular, rosy-cheeked baby dykes who won't mind carting them around and will take an interest in their constantly repeated stories about the old days, the bars, the music festivals. The women's restaurants. There was one, Ralfie had taken a date there, and the dessert, some sort of nondairy cheese concoction, tasted really off, burnt or something. So Ralfie waved over the waitress, but instead of discreetly sneaking it back to the kitchen, the waitress gathered the whole collective to their table and passed the plate around, each *restaurateuse* claiming in turn, "Tastes okay to me." "Me too." "Nothing wrong with this." And they refused to take it off the bill. That's lesbians for you, Ralfie thinks admiringly. Sticking to their guns.

Fat chance of a baby dyke, she realizes. Who would want to do that? The reality is, they'll have to pay someone, and where all that money will come from, she doesn't know. They'll have to keep working to afford it—but if they're healthy enough to keep working, they won't need it. Ha ha.

Ralfie climbs into the truck and revs it a few times as the guys pile in. Since she's been back, they've made her the driver. It used to be Shawn, but they're all relieved not to have him skidding around corners anymore or burning rubber as he pulls away from the stop lights.

16

Silence

The silence between Dot and Ralfie has gone on for an entire week, and it's making them both miserable, so on Saturday morning after breakfast, Dot forces herself to break it: "We have to talk."

"Now?" Ralfie whines.

"I think so," says Dot. "Yeah."

"I was on my way to the gym!" Ralfie ostentatiously starts unlacing her sneakers. How to wreck a perfectly good weekend. Dot's right, she understands. They have to talk. But do they have to do it this minute? Unfortunately she can't come up with an alternative minute. Any time is bad. She can always think of something more interesting to do than have a capital-T Talk. Even, say, balancing the checkbook. Ralfie would rather balance the checkbook than have this Talk. She would rather go to the dentist! At least with a drill in her mouth, she wouldn't be expected to discuss anything. "I was only trying to be realistic," she says, realizing that having a capital-T talk instead of going to the gym means that at least she won't have to manage the stairs. "One of us has to."

This is incredibly annoying, since it's Dot who has innumerable times brought them down to earth. Even now, look at her, jumping into the breach, while Ralfie would have let the silence go on indefinitely. Until Dot did something about it. As she just has. Dot takes a breath and tries to put all that aside. "I know, baby," she attempts. "But . . ."

"But what?"

"But—Maple Grave? It isn't anything like what I imagined for us. For myself. Why should we have to uproot ourselves? We paid on this place for years, we know the neighbors, we like walking around the pond. The store around the corner is so convenient."

"It's a dump."

"Come on, it's not that bad. So they could sweep the floor more often. What if you had to get in the car just to pick up a quart of milk?"

"The milk from that store goes bad. I think they buy it at a discount when it's past its sell-by date."

"Nobody does that, it would be illegal." *How can she let Ralfie distract her like this?* Dot thinks, annoyed with herself. "And that's beside the point. We're getting off the subject."

"Just saying. That store isn't much of an argument"—Ralfie starts taking things out of her gym bag and lining them up on the kitchen table: earphones, a packet of shoelaces, two balls of socks, a pair of panties, a bra— "for staying up here, in the penthouse."

"Please do not put your nasty gym stuff on the table," says Dot in a monotone, like a robot programmed to repeat this sentence.

"I just thought I'd see what needs washing. Jeez. Sorry." Ralfie sweeps it all onto the floor. "And don't have a conniption fit. I'll put it away later. After we finish our big talk."

"I don't know what I imagined, really," Dot persists, forcing herself to ignore Ralfie's attitude and her stuff, which she's obviously thrown on the floor just to bug her. "I guess I thought we'd just go on like we were, and then at some point we'd keel over." Hearing herself say this, Dot realizes it's ridiculous, adolescent. "Don't tell me you didn't think so too."

"Maybe," says Ralfie. Dot catches her eye. "A little."

"Anyway, we can't afford to retire, and we don't want to anyway—"

"I don't need to retire if I can just get up and down the freaking stairs," Ralfie bursts out. "What happens when I have to get the other knee done?"

"Oh," says Dot. "That's what this is all about."

"Yes, that's what this is all about! What else would it be? I don't think you're trying to see things from my point of view!"

"I thought that was way in the future. The other knee."

"Well, it's not. It's throbbing and clicking all the time."

"I didn't know."

"You could've asked."

"No, I couldn't," says Dot, exasperated. "You get mad and refuse to talk about it whenever anyone brings it up. But it's just the stairs. We like everything else about living here, right? There has to be something we can do about them."

"Like what?" says Ralfie. "Install a slide?"

The image makes Dot laugh. The children at the library would love it. *Ms. Greenbaum has a slide in her house!* Jim would too, he's such a kid. "How about a fire pole?" she says.

"Not funny!" says Ralfie. "And they're not *just* stairs. We're on them all day, if you haven't noticed. Up, down, up, down. No wonder I have bad knees. I'm surprised you don't too."

"It's different for me." Every once in a while, climbing to their floor, Dot experiences that strange breathlessness and remembers the weight on her chest, the inability to inhale. "You probably notice the stairs more because of your knees. What if we get one of those chairlift things?"

"Dotty, have you looked at our stairs? They wind around. You need a straight-up flight for a chairlift. And we'd have to get the neighbors to agree to it. And they're a fire hazard. I've already sussed this out. There's nothing we can do."

Dot's cornered. The chairlift looks so convenient in the TV ads, the gray-haired gentleman riding up with a relieved smile on his face as his wife watches from the foot of the stairs. Dot thinks of him as English, for some reason—maybe it's his cardigan—and she realizes Ralfie's right: a lift probably wouldn't fit on a normal, American staircase, or if it did, it would probably break down all the time, like the elevators in the subway. She hears the announcements sometimes, although they're so garbled you can hardly understand them, and she wonders what you do if you're merrily riding the train in your wheelchair, and suddenly you find out that the elevator at your stop is out of service, and you're stuck on the Green Street platform. Do you just have to wait around until it's fixed? Are there wheelchair users riding underground forever, like Charlie in the old song, hoping to find a working lift?

Dot never imagined she would think this about her own life, but she's not getting any younger. Ralfie neither. Which is something her mother would have said. She admits, "I looked at that building down the street. The senior housing one?"

"What did you do that for?" says Ralfie. "You either have to be dead broke, which fortunately we are not, or you pay through the nose!"

"So you knew that already."

"Me and the guys have been over there a million times. Place is a wreck." Ralfie leans over from her chair and starts gathering her gym things off the floor. "I mean, I don't know what we should do either, baby. But a chairlift, or some old skyscraper—that just ain't us."

"And Maple Grove is?"

"No, okay? It's not. I had a moment of insanity—"

"Caused by the pain in your knees," Dot jokes cautiously.

"We'll just stay here until we croak, and then the city can put us out with the trash, how about that?"

"Sounds good," says Dot. This talk has solved exactly nothing! Although at least she and Ralfie are back on speaking terms.

Ralfie's just relieved that the talk is over. "So, do you have anything for the wash?"

"No, thanks, honey. But I'll do the shopping if you help me make a list," Dot offers.

17

Dot Drags Herself

When Dot drags herself to work, seeing the children again is cheering, as she had hoped. It's pulling her out of her black hole, inch by inch, even when she clings, resistant, to the walls. "They're better than Prozac," she admits to Jim. Actually, Dot's never taken Prozac, although Susan and her cardiologist and even Ralfie have all urged antidepressants on her at one time or another. She's not really sure why she's so opposed, but it has something to do with a fear that the pills would eradicate her essential Dot-ness and then be hard to kick if she doesn't like them. She wants to be all there, to feel whatever she's feeling, even if it's lousy. "I should've come back weeks ago."

"I don't know about that," says Jim. "It sounds like you were pretty sick." He regales everyone during their breaks with stories of his dates with the boys he meets online—but it's all a persona he's trying out. Most of the time he can't help showing his actual shyness, and Dot can tell he finds her condition—her morning silences and her lunchtime medication lineup—scary. No doubt he thinks it's far from anything he'll have to deal with in his own life. All she can say to that is, *Just wait.*

While Dot was out sick, Jim streaked his hair magenta and chartreuse, and the dye must have leached out the natural oils, or something, because now it sits on top of his head like a garish bird's nest, which can't be the effect he was aiming for. Can it?

At first the children are timid around her. Jim reminds them who she is: "She's our old friend, Ms. Greenbaum!"

"I think maybe she used to be here," admits Niecey, a quiet child whose elaborate cornrows indicate her patient, obedient nature.

"Of course she was! She's my boss, you know," Jim explains. "Ms. Greenbaum is the big cheese!"

"A cheese?"

"What's *boss*?"

"You dumbass. The boss is the boss of everybody!" shouts Moe. With his blond crewcut and his squarish body, it's already apparent he'll be a fullback in high school.

"He said a swear! He called me a swear!" complains Niecey excitedly. "He's stupid, right, Mr. Tran?"

"Wrong," sighs Jim. "Nobody should call anybody names. Saying 'stupid' is as bad as swearing."

"Think about how you would feel," Dot tells Niecey, backing Jim up, "if someone called you stupid."

"But that's not a swear," Niecey insists. "My mom would wash his mouth out with soap!"

"She would?" asks Dot. Did parents actually do this? Is it something she should report? "Really, sweetheart?" she tries to confirm.

"Uh-uh. It's just a thing she says."

"Mine too!"

"I'd get a time out!"

The children want to touch Jim's hair, and to move everyone on from the morality of swearing, and soap, he kneels down to let them. He's good, playful and empathic, thinks Dot as she watches the children pat his hair. They love him, probably more than they love her, she thinks enviously, since even to win their approval, she's not about to start rolling around on the floor. They wouldn't forget Jim if he was out sick for a month.

"Mr. Tran is a clown," one child explains to the rest, as though this is a singular, permanent identity.

"Cute," says Jim. Then Moe starts tugging at Jim's bangs, like he's trying remove them. "Ow! Quit that!"

"Story time!" calls Dot, taking charge.

"Yay!"

"I call *Wild Things!*"

"No, I hate that one. It has monsters."

"Baby, baby, you are a baby!" a child sings.

Jim stands, and the children follow him to the story circle like imprinted chicks. He is right, they are so cute and sweet, thinks Dot. When they're not pulling hair. And even that's not so bad, compared to the harm adults do to one another. She smiles down at them. Their little faces. It feels like trying to do an exercise she hasn't done in months.

18

The Particular Quiet
of the Closed Library

Dot has always liked to arrive at her office early, to drink coffee and read the newspaper in the particular quiet of the closed library, even an elementary school library like this one. A persistent buzzing from her phone startles her, and she checks the screen to see a rebus of pictographs and acronyms that she's about to delete when she realizes it's from Germaine. Perhaps, Dot thinks, she's resorted to these hieroglyphics because she doesn't know enough English words.

"But, no!" explains Germaine when Dot calls her back. "This is the universal language of texting. I thought everyone understood."

So it's not a language barrier, between her and Germaine, but an age one. The emojis remind Dot of the codes people like her and Ralfie used back in the day, to recognize each other. They were "friends of Dorothy" and "members of the tribe." They shamelessly wore green on Thursdays—or was it Fridays?—and lavender any time. They dropped hairpins and spilled tea. They knew the dish. Now it's all gone mainstream. People come out of the closet over just about anything, from a diagnosis of cancer to a decision to go vegan—and the phrase barely applies to being gay, since that's not much of a reveal anymore. She supposes this means she'll have to learn to read texts, since at least according to Germaine, everybody else can. "'Sup?" she asks—Jim's greeting every morning when he arrives.

"*Comment?*" says Germaine.

"What did you want to talk about?"

"Ah," says Germaine. "Susan has made a deposit on a condo in Maple Grove. Do you know this?"

Dot is shocked. "She threatened to, but I didn't think she really meant it," she says slowly.

"Not the one we visited, it is bigger and with a back deck. She wants to have a *barbecue*. This is something new to me."

"It's probably too cold for cooking out, up there in Quebec."

"We are not at the North Pole, Dotty! But we do not eat sitting with the plates in our laps. I am not *down with* Susan's idea, you know? My job is here, my teaching. My friends. In Maple Grove, I would be very isolated. And driving all the time in bad traffic."

"I agree," says Dot. "I don't know why Susan is doing this."

"You agree? I am so happy to hear this! Susan said something different—"

"That sneak! What did she tell you?"

"Well, she didn't tell, exactly. But I thought you are coming too. And my husband!"

"Your husband?" asks Dot, trying not to sound too intrigued.

"Ha, you know! Mr. Belrose."

"Oh. Ralfie."

"Yes, he is so sweet. She. She is so sweet."

That's a new facet of Ralfie's personality, Dot thinks.

"So, you will persuade Susan not to move? I like her very much, but I don't think our relationship will work if she is in the old-age home—"

"It's not an old-age home. Why does everybody say that? It's a development—"

"And she wants me to come with her. But I am too young, and you know, broke. Teaching French does not pay so much. And the students who learned in France do not like my accent, they are Parisian snobs. Maybe I will get fired."

"Germaine, I'm truly sorry for your problems, but I've never persuaded Susan of anything in my life," says Dot. "I don't think anyone has."

"But you, her sister, you will talk to her, okay?" says Germaine. "I am so grateful. I would be so sad if Susan leaves me. She's so good to me, and sexy, and we—"

"Germaine," Dot interrupts. She doesn't want to hear about Susan's sexual technique.

"I know, I know, I should not bother you at work, but I don't know what to do. That sign on the highway, I wish I never saw it. It is bad news."

"That's right, I forgot you started all this," says Dot.

"Not me!" says Germaine. "I thought it was for you. Susan and I, we were together only six months. I didn't know her so well. I didn't realize she is so old."

"Okay, okay, I'll give it a try," Dot promises. She adds "call Susan" to a mental list that also includes "call Viola" and "cook dinner." It's a depressing list. She decides to make a meatloaf and texts Ralfie to ask her to take the chopped turkey out of the freezer. If Dot knew what she was doing, she probably could just send her a little picture of a meatloaf. Ralfie texts back kissy lips.

"Does that mean you're taking out the chopped meat?" Dot asks.

Ralfie sends a thumbs-up.

Soon we'll all go around grunting, thinks Dot. Maybe it will be an improvement. Actual conversations never seem to solve anything—look at her and Ralfie. When they don't create more problems, you're lucky.

19

Ralfie Falls Out of a Tree

Ralfie falls out of a tree. She doesn't fall far—it's a small tree. But it's far enough that she blacks out briefly when she lands, and opens her eyes to find herself lying face down in the dirt, able to remember that before she was there, she was in a tree, but unable to remember why. It's late in the afternoon, and the ground is cold. She tries to roll over but is stopped by a familiar, excruciating pain in her knee—the surgically enhanced one. "Not again," she groans.

"Are you in pain?" Shawn asks hopefully. He's taken a few first-aid classes, and he's always looking for a chance to show off how much he knows. This is the initial question he's been taught to ask, as a first responder.

"Of course I am, asshole!" says Ralfie.

"Good, you're breathing. Just try to relax," he says, with unexpected kindness.

Maybe this is why Clarice puts up with him, Ralfie thinks.

Carefully, he repositions her. "The ambulance is on its way."

Nelson, the only Black man on the crew, is a burly, light-skinned Jamaican, nicknamed Nellie, although somehow this never leads to jokes, perhaps because of his intimidating size yet peaceable demeanor. Noticing Ralfie's disorientation, he reminds her, "We were taking down the Christmas lights."

"We were?" says Ralfie. "What month is it?"

"March," says Nelson. "That's why. They should've come down already. You're just a little shaken up—happens to everyone."

"You leaned over too far, you should've moved the ladder," explains Shawn.

"Yeah, like you ever bothered to move the ladder," says Ralfie.

"Yeah, like I'm not the one who fell. You shouldn't have been up there anyway—"

"Don't tell me what to do—"

"Next time I'll get the lights," says Nelson. "I'm big enough, I don't need to move the ladder."

"Right," says Shawn. "The gentle giant."

"I don't like that name," says Nelson.

"The jolly green giant, then."

"Drop it, man, unless you want to see my gentle side."

"Dot's going to kill me," says Ralfie. Her knee is throbbing, and her head has started throbbing along in time.

"She might—" says Shawn.

"Nah, she won't," Nelson interrupts. "How could you think that? She'll be worried to death. I know *my* friend would . . ." He stops himself. Ralfie and the guys have figured out all about Nelson's "friend," and they've noticed how he never takes overtime but is always eager to knock off and go home to him—but Nelson doesn't get it. They're fine with his home life. They've been dealing with Ralfie all these years.

And of course Nelson is right. Dot is frantic. Speeding to the emergency room, she tries to put their conversation about the stairs out of her mind and to repress her anxiety about *what now*. If Ralfie's okay, Dot tells herself, that's all that matters. We'll figure out the rest.

Ralfie's ortho, when he examines Ralfie at the hospital the next day, is the one who's furious. "I did a beautiful job on this knee and now look at it," he says.

"If it was so beautiful, why did I fall?" says Ralfie. "It was unstable."

"Of course you have certain limitations! What did you think you were doing?"

"My job! You didn't say anything about trees."

"For chrissake. What seventy-year-old climbs a tree?"

"Sixty-eight!" says Ralfie.

Listening to this conversation, Dot sighs with relief. Ralfie is Ralfie.

"We're going to have to do another surgery," says the doctor. "And this time I can't guarantee the outcome."

"Oh, honey," says Dot. "I'm so sorry. This is bad."

"*You're* sorry? *He's* the one who should be sorry." Ralfie sounds close to tears.

"I *am* sorry—for you, Ms. Greenbaum. I'm sorry you have such an irrational wife. Patients like her can be very difficult to deal with. But we will do our best, right?"

Dot resists the alliance he is trying to make, although she knows she should try to appease him. "My *wife*," she says with dignity, "has an injured knee and a concussion. She's disoriented and in pain. Please don't scold her."

"Dot's right!" says Ralfie. "Your bedside manner sucks."

The doctor looks shocked. "I may have to ask you to find another orthopedist," he says.

"Oh, no, please, Doctor," Dot begs. He's obnoxious, but he already understands Ralfie's knee situation, and they picked him originally because he's supposed to be the best. The best of the best. The idea of searching for someone else makes her head hurt. Can't the guy just do his job, like everyone else in the world, without expecting them to pay homage? "She's just a little traumatized right now. Like I said. She has a low pain threshold—"

"What do you mean?" Ralfie interrupts, insulted. "I can take as much as the next guy."

The next guy with a prescription, Dot thinks.

The doctor, who seems to have decided to avoid tangling with Ralfie, addresses Dot. "Okay, Ms. Greenbaum, but from now on, both of you, please try to control yourselves. I'd like to maintain an amicable therapeutic relationship," he says, clearly looking forward to the moment when the anesthesiologist comes in and knocks Ralfie out. "The surgery is scheduled for tomorrow. I was able to fit her in, because of her emergent situation— fractured patella. We'll do what we can."

Dot doesn't even bother to ask what he's talking about. More words, she thinks.

When the doctor is gone, Ralfie says, "Well, I guess I can stop worrying about the other knee."

"For now," says Dot.

"It feels great compared to this one. Who would've thought a little fall would cause so much damage?"

"Most people?" says Dot. "I hate to say it, honey, but the doc is right, you have to accept some limitations."

"I've had way worse accidents than this—"

"Maybe, but you can't risk them anymore," says Dot. She's not sure how Ralfie will take this, but she adds, "Your knee repair's too fragile."

Ralfie tries to take it as a joke. "That's me," says Ralfie. "A delicate flower. Come here and give your fragile girl a hug."

Dot lies down on the hospital bed, careful not to jostle Ralfie's leg, and embraces her. They hold each other close, each trying to comfort the other, each worrying in her own way.

20

There's Ralfie. Again.

So there's Ralfie. Again. Stuck on the living room couch in her knee surgery outfit—DPW hoody, Valentine's Day boxers.

The contraption holding her leg together this time looks even more complicated than the previous one. It includes a metal brace, with a circular hinge at the side of the knee, and it weighs a ton—which has the virtue, Dot's realized, of keeping Ralfie nearly immobilized and unable to get up without some assistance and rove the apartment with her walker, in search of sedatives. Before Dot leaves for work, she prepares Ralfie's lunch and puts it within reach on the coffee table, next to a stack of mysteries, Ralfie's laptop, and the TV clicker. Even with these amusements, though, most days when Dot comes home, Ralfie's asleep.

"This is boring!" she complains. "I can't stand it. Why doesn't Shelly come more often? At least with her I have something to do."

"You can't do therapy all the time," says Dot, trying to be reasonable. "You're also supposed to rest. Anyway, I thought you didn't like Shelly—"

"She's fine," Ralfie cuts her off. "And aren't I supposed to be moving around more, so I don't lose my muscle tone? It's bad enough that I haven't been to the gym—"

"I don't know, honey—"

"I hate resting!" says Ralfie. "And my knee hurts. And I have to pee."

"Don't have a tantrum," says Dot.

"You try it," grumbles Ralfie.

Dot brings Ralfie her walker and helps her move from lying to sitting. "Put your good foot down and lean on the walker," Dot reminds her. She spots Ralfie as she stands and positions herself on the walker and hops with it to the bathroom. Dot puts together a bag of ice and piles some pillows on the coffee table.

"Put your foot up here and let me wrap the ice around your knee," Dot tells her when she comes back. "It'll feel a lot better."

"Oxy'd be faster."

"Forget it. The doctor only gave you a couple of pills, and you used them up days ago. I can give you a tylenol."

"I'll take what I can get," says Ralfie. She really does wish she could knock herself out. She hasn't been using the computer to play games, as she's told Dot. She's been reading up on patella breaks, and the news is not good. None of the websites say anything about what happens if you break the bone after you've already had the knee repaired, but the break is bad enough by itself. The doc didn't even bother to pretend that her leg would be *good as new*. Desk job, here I come, she thinks disconsolately. She doesn't know how long she'll be able to tolerate being a bureaucrat. And retiring on disability sounds only slightly less boring than sitting around, recovering from a knee operation. Not to mention the money problems it would cause.

Dot's been reading the same websites and having the same sorts of thoughts. *Maybe this is what aging is*, she thinks. Small things become big things. Or rather, there are no small things. It's like when you're a kid. A step taken, a shoelace tied, a word on the page—everything's a revelation. Except now, everything's an obstacle. A loss of footing, a little shortness of breath, and you can't just jump back up and keep running anymore. Instead, your life is wrecked.

Dot points the clicker at the TV. "Let's watch a movie," she says. "Something black and white and romantic."

For once, Ralfie goes along with this. Dot breaks out the microwave popcorn and they watch *Casablanca* for the millionth time. "Ah, we'll always have knee surgery," says Ralfie when it's over, and Dot laughs through her movie tears—Hollywood gets her every time—but it's true, the crisis has brought them closer, in a way. They haven't exactly discussed it, but they both know they're facing a big, new kind of obstacle. If only there was a plane coming to fly them to safety at the end.

"I think I'll get a fedora like Ingrid's," says Dot.

"Me too!" says Ralfie.

"Don't you dare," says Dot. "We *cannot* start wearing the same clothes."

"But we'll wear them differently. We won't look alike at all!"

"No way!" says Dot. "Anyway, you can't get out to buy a fedora if I refuse to help you."

"I'll order it online."

"Cheater!"

"Control freak!"

In the old days—meaning Before Surgeries—this would have become an enjoyable wrestling match on the couch, but that's impossible now. Dot says, "Let's go to bed, baby," and fetches Ralfie's walker, although she wonders how they'll manage with Ralfie's movement so limited. "Let's play big butch and flirty femme."

"But who'll be who?" says Ralfie.

Although Dot thinks that's obvious, they end up taking turns.

21

Viola Calls

Viola calls Dot. "Aren't we due for one of our lunches? I've missed you!"

"I'm so glad you asked." Finally, thinks Dot, a conversation she doesn't have to initiate. This is why one needs a girlfriend who's older and hopefully wiser. Plus, she has something she wants to ask Viola about. "The Indian place?"

"Natch," says Viola, who enjoys using the slang of her youth. Or maybe it's her mother's youth. When they get to the restaurant and are settled into their table, and the haughty waiter serves them dishes that aren't exactly what they ordered, she says, "Although I don't know why we keep coming here."

"Habit?" says Dot. "And the food's not bad, whatever it turns out to be." When the waiter comes around to collect their plates, they reject dessert menus—offerings like rosewater milk balls or syrup toast never sound enticing.

"Sweets are so culture-specific," says Viola. "Look at the Japanese and their bean paste."

"We'll just have tea," Dot tells the waiter. "Cream and sugar, please." He brings the tea just as she ordered it—which is not how they take it, they both like lemon, but Dot thought she had finally learned how to manage this restaurant. Only with the tea does she introduce her big topic. "Ralfie wants to move," she says.

"No!" says Viola.

"Yes!"

"But I thought you loved your aerie—"

"I do! But Ralfie—"

"It's unfortunate that the elderly housing near you is so impossible," Viola muses. Dot has told her about her walk. "I don't know who can afford to live there. People who don't need to, I suppose."

"Even before she fell, she was complaining, and now? It's a production, getting her in and out of the building." Dot hesitates, forces herself to admit, "It's not easy for me, either. Some days I'm out of breath at the first landing. But I can deal with that! Ralfie, though—"

"There must be some solution. What about one of those chairlift contraptions they're always advertising during the TV news?"

Dot sighs. "We've been over all that. Our stairs wind around too much. And anyway, those chairlifts probably break all the time, don't you think?"

"I suppose it doesn't do to depend on a mechanical device. But why is it always advertised during the news? Are there an exceptional number of disabled people who watch it? I've always wondered—"

"They advertise drugs too. Old people, like us, watch the news."

"I suppose," says Viola distractedly, and continues, "But you've both made such wonderful progress. You with your walking regimen and Ralfie with her PT. Don't you think the problem's just temporary—"

"Viola," Dot interrupts. She's getting the feeling that Viola senses where this conversation is going and is trying to head it off. "Do you know if there are any vacancies in your building? Would you put in a good word for us?"

Viola shakes her head. "For an intelligent woman, you can be very naive. Do you realize how long I've lived in that apartment? I was still working full time! I could never afford to buy it now."

"Oh," says Dot, wondering if she has to cross off this possibility on her mental list. It's not much of a list, actually. There's nothing else on it.

"Never," Viola repeats. "The people moving in now? Young. Singles, couples. I don't know how they manage it. Their parents, I suppose. Or perhaps they have jobs in *high tech*." She emphasizes the phrase, as though it's in a foreign language she has just mastered. "I get calls daily from real estate agents, waving money at me."

"Oh," Dot says again.

"Figuratively, of course. Whenever one of us oldsters goes, the workmen are in there, practically the next day, banging away. Refurbishing, you know."

"That's just rude," says Dot. They've finished their imperfect tea, so she signals for the check.

"Feelings, *politesse*, mean nothing to them," says Viola. "Although I suppose the renovations are nice enough. Anyway, you must realize it would be quite awkward, Ralfie and me in such proximity, day after day. Even though you and I haven't been, well, lately—"

"Ralfie doesn't know anything about all that, Vi! She's never asked a single question about us. She trusts me."

"Really," states Viola.

"Yes, really! It's not an issue, if that's what you're worried about."

"I suppose the awkwardness would dissipate over time, although I don't know why Ralfie trusts you about something like this—"

"Of course she does! And I trust her."

"Listen to yourself, Dotty! We've been fooling around quite pleasantly all these years, yet you think Ralfie should trust you!"

"I do! What's between you and me is different. It's got nothing to do with Ralfie."

Viola looks skeptical. "In any case, my dear, that's all beside the point. The fact is, you can't afford my building, and neither could I, if I were in your shoes."

22

Dot Does Her Duties

Dot does her morning homecare duties efficiently, positioning a lunch box for Ralfie, a few back issues of *Sports Illustrated*, and the computer next to the couch. Ralfie won't need to drag herself around the apartment unless she needs to pee, and Dot can't do anything about that. She looks forward to her quiet time, but this morning, when she arrives at the library, Jim is already there, distraught, as she's never seen him. His hair, at least the magenta half of it, is literally standing on end.

"You're here so early, Ms. Greenbaum," he says. "My lucky day. Ha ha. Well, no, it isn't. But maybe you'll have some idea—probably not though."

"You can call me Dot." Dot tries to calm him. "'Ms. Greenbaum' is for the kids." How well does she know this boy, really? Must she solve his problems, whatever they are? At his age, it's probably a disappointing date or a flat tire, or something equally non-momentous that will be forgotten by tomorrow.

"Dot," he repeats. "Dot. It's my parents. They're in serious trouble."

"Your parents?" says Dot. "I don't understand. What kind of trouble could your parents get into?" She imagines a diminutive, gray-haired couple— doll-like, wearing identical wire-rimmed glasses, the sun reflecting from the lenses so you can't see their eyes, bowing to strangers on the street. The strangers ignore them. The image is racist, she realizes, shaking her head to banish it. She must have it all wrong. Maybe they've been hawking impotence cures made from rhinoceros tusks. More racism.

"My mom got a ticket for making a right on red. She's such a cautious driver, but she couldn't see the sign. It was hidden by a tree."

"She should appeal it!" says Dot. "Did she take a picture?"

"No, no, my parents don't want any trouble. They paid the ticket right away. But now my mom won't leave the house. She's worried about the immigration police."

"Should she be?" asks Dot. This problem is way outside her experience. She's lived in Boston all her life, and so have most of the people she knows, she realizes. There's Germaine—but she's Canadian, practically American. Although there is all that French.

"They have green cards. And they won't talk to me about this stuff. All they say is, 'Don't worry, you are fine. Our all-American boy.' Christ!"

"But if they have green cards, shouldn't they be okay? Maybe they don't understand our laws."

Jim looks annoyed. "They probably understand more than you. They've been dealing with the fucking immigration service forever. And now Trump. I don't know." Jim pulls at his hair, making it stick up even more. "Maybe it's finally driven them crazy. My mom claims you can be deported if you break the law. 'Green card don't matter,' she says."

"But—for a moving violation?" says Dot.

"*I* don't think so. But try convincing her. She just says, 'Trump will cancel our cards. Deport everybody!' Ever since she got that ticket, she's become completely paranoid. She quit her job! How are they supposed to support themselves?"

"What about your father—can't he do something?"

"Him? He's backing her up! He wants me to come home and help him with the shopping! He says, 'For your mommy, Son. Just until this blows over.' But I know him—that could be years! How will I finish my internship? My degree? My life is over!"

"Don't be so dramatic," says Dot. "Calm down." Although she doesn't really know why he should. Maybe his parents are paranoid—but maybe they have a point. Probably both. "Let's try to figure something out. Isn't that what you wanted to ask me?"

"No, I've gotta run, or they'll start calling me again. I'll be out for the rest of the day. Or maybe forever!"

Jim rushes out of the room before Dot can say more—not that she has anything to offer. Poor guy.

23

Ralfie Gets a Bad Feeling

Ralfie's getting a bad feeling about her knee. She's been working with Shelly again, but it's different. The first time around, Ralfie resisted and teased, but she did the exercises Shelly prescribed, and after a while, they worked. Her pain went away, or at least diminished. Shelly discharged her, and Ralfie went back to work on the truck. This time, though, Shelly looks worried.

"Life getting you down? Boyfriend?" asks Ralfie. "Girlfriend?" she adds hopefully.

"What?" says Shelly. "No, nothing like that." She tries to smile at her client, but her brow knits right up again.

"Then what?" asks Ralfie.

Shelly hesitates. She's always carrying around a lot of paperwork, and she pulls a chart from one of her folders. "See these lines?" She shows Ralfie. "The red one tracks your progress last time. The blue one is this time."

"But the blue's way under the red," says Ralfie.

"Exactly," says Shelly.

"But I'm working harder—"

"You're not recovering like I expected." She sighs. "And I've run out of ideas. I'm going to ask my supervisor. She's more experienced, she might have some suggestions."

"If she doesn't?" Ralfie says, feeling suddenly dizzy.

"I don't know. I hate to say it, but your doc said there was a lot of damage."

"But what's he know?" Ralfie says, somewhat hysterically. "Right?"

Shelly puts the chart back in the folder and gathers up her things. "I'll be back next week, and I'll let you know if I learn anything new. In the meantime, keep doing the exercises we went over. The leg lifts and all."

Ralfie nods, not trusting herself to speak. This might be the worst news anyone's ever given her, outside of a death in the family or something.

How will she tell Dot? She can't imagine saying it. She tries it out: "My knee . . ." She can't continue. Tries again, just to herself, in her mind. A practice shot. *My knee is not getting better. My knee is not going to get better.* No. "My knee . . ." She still can't say it.

When Dot gets home, Ralfie is propped up on her pillow, poking at her computer. She looks up and catches Dot's eye. To anyone else, maybe, Ralfie would look the same as always, but Dot can tell. She can feel it. "What happened?" She panics. "Did you fall?"

Ralfie tries out the phrase she practiced. "My knee . . . ," she attempts.

"Honey, I can't understand you. Are you sick?"

Ralfie takes a deep breath, holds it in for a moment, and blurts out, "*My-knee-is-never-getting-better.*"

"What? How do you know? You don't know that—"

"Shelly showed me. She has a graph."

"Oh, a graph. Big deal," says Dot with relief. She sits down next to Ralfie. "The kid's just trying to impress you with her scientific know-how."

"No, Shelly's right. I knew it, even before she said anything."

"You did not! You told me it was going great, you'd be up and about in a few weeks!"

"Denial, baby," says Ralfie sadly. "I don't know why you listen to me. I'll keep trying and all, but—I've been thinking, lying here. I was right before. We can't stay in this place. We've been dreaming."

"I asked Viola about her building, the other day when we had lunch, but—"

"Wait! You what?" cries Ralfie. "Why didn't you tell me? That is brilliant!" *You just never know*, she thinks. Viola is absolutely the last person she would have wanted to come to their rescue, and she has her reasons for feeling that way. But a South End high-rise. An elevator—she would probably have to make small talk with the neighbors. And she would have to be supercareful, walking on the historic brick sidewalks. But so what? She could get around.

"No, no!" says Dot. "It's no good. Viola said—"

Ralfie ignores her, reaches out to take her in her arms. "Give us a hug. You're a genius!"

"You can't be serious," says Dot, wiggling out of Ralfie's embrace. "I didn't tell you because Viola nearly laughed me out of the restaurant. We don't have that kind of money. Viola said she could never afford to buy there now."

"Dotty, listen. We sell this place, cash in our IRAs, maybe borrow some from your sister—"

"She just bought Maple Grave! She doesn't have any money, not now!"

"Whatever, we put it together—"

"Who burns through their savings at our age?" Dot can't believe where this conversation is going.

"It's an investment! Property! It's solid. Better than a dumb IRA!"

"I don't understand you," says Dot. "Don't you think you're just having a bad day?"

Ralfie snorts. "A bad year, more like," she says. "You're always such a comfort."

"What do you want from me?" Dot bursts out. "We'll have nothing! How you think we'll pay some gigantic mortgage, even if we could get one, I have no idea!"

Ralfie sits up, smooths Dot's hair, puts her arm around Dot's shoulder. "Dotty, Dotty, honey. How did we get like this?"

Dot shrugs. "I'm tired," she says. "And you just said I shouldn't listen to you."

"But we can do this, I told you—"

"You really believe that?" Dot looks at Ralfie skeptically.

"I do, absolutely. Just think it over, for me—"

"You're amazing," says Dot.

Later that evening, trying to read a book, Dot feels short of breath, she can't seem to fully inhale, and she wonders if she's having another heart attack. She's not. In a bizarre way, it's wishful thinking. She would pass out and be carried to the hospital, and someone else would have to figure things out for a change. But her symptoms are just anxiety.

Maybe we could hire Nelson and Shawn to carry Ralfie up and down the stairs, she thinks. They're strong. Dot herself can still manage, not always easily, but she hasn't yet had to sit down and rest before making it to their floor. They would probably find the offer insulting. And she can just imagine Ralfie's outrage. It's a ridiculous idea, and it wouldn't solve anything, anyway—the stairs are only part of the problem. Symbolic. But also real.

24

"What?"

Ralfie's phone rings, waking her from her postprandial nap. "What?" she says impatiently.

"You'd think you're actually busy or something," says Shawn. "Nelson and I took the afternoon off, thought we'd come visit."

"Why not?" says Ralfie. They're usually good for a laugh, and they'll take her mind off things. Dot's still intransigent; she's become a total tightwad, Ralfie thinks. You have to spend money to make money! Everybody knows that. Ralfie's made an appointment with the financial advisor at the bank. She's checking out the possibilities.

Dot hid a key on the front porch, under a flowerpot containing a pathetic gray plant, so when Ralfie has visitors, she doesn't have to somehow get down the stairs to let them in. Shawn and Nelson clomp up the stairs, and Shawn drops a six-pack on the coffee table. "From us and the guys," he says, extricating a can and popping it open. "A little get-well present."

"Nice of you," says Ralfie. "Can I have one?"

Nelson hands her a beer and takes one for himself. "How're you doing, girl?" he asks.

Ralfie takes a sip. "Ahh," she says. "Sometimes a crummy old Bud really hits the spot." She points at her leg. "As far as that goes, you can see how I'm doing. Sucky."

"So, when do you think you'll be back on the truck?" asks Shawn.

Ralfie shrugs. "Don't know." She shakes her head, tries not to let her eyes fill. "The doc says he's—quote unquote—not optimistic. Asshole."

"Right. Asshole!" Shawn crumples his beer can and drops it on the coffee table, takes another, waves the remaining two cans at Ralfie and Nelson. "Want?"

"Whoa, take it easy," says Nelson. "Don't go bogarting them all." He turns to Ralfie. "You know, there's people, the doctors told them they'd never walk again, now they're running marathons."

"Exactly!" says Ralfie, although she doesn't believe this, or at least doesn't believe she is one of those people. "That's exactly what I tell Dot. The poor kid believes whatever they tell her."

"But what do *you* think?" asks Nelson.

Ralfie shrugs, and the three are silent. She takes another beer and hands the last one to Nelson.

"Check this out," Shawn bursts out. "You know Margaret O'Connell? In the office downtown? She retired."

"Good for her," says Ralfie.

"You know what her job was?"

"Uh, no—should I?"

"Yeah, you should. She ran the complaint department."

"Sounds like a barrel of laughs," says Ralfie. "For some old bat."

"No, listen. People used to email her about all kinds of shit. She showed me the forms. One guy checked off 'Dead animal' and wrote, 'Flat cat.'" He laughs. "Flat cat! You'd get a charge out of it, reading that stuff all day, sending us guys out to scrape animals off the sidewalk. Boston drivers— they don't care what they run into."

"You're a psycho!" says Ralfie. "Dead animals. That's sick."

"Potholes, trees down," says Nelson. "You'd be, like, a dispatcher. It's not a bad gig."

"It's not the truck," says Ralfie.

"The great outdoors," says Shawn.

"The snow, the rain, the heat," says Nelson. "The injuries—"

"I'll think about it." Ralfie cuts him off. "Did you bring any more beer? This stuff goes right through you."

"Nah," says Nelson. "We just brought you a taste."

"Well, one of you needs to give me a hand," says Ralfie. She sits up and swings her legs around to the floor. "I used to do this at the gym," she says. "One-legged stands from the bench. With weights in my hands."

"That was then," says Nelson. "Use your hands to push yourself up." She stands, wobbles, balances herself. Nelson grabs her walker and positions it in front of her. "There you go."

"Thanks, pal," she says. Leaning on it, she limps to the bathroom.

"Phew," says Shawn. "Not an easy life."

"Uh-uh," Nelson agrees. "That truck won't be the same without her."

"You really think she won't be back?"

"Don't look like it," says Nelson. People don't listen to him, but he usually knows what he's talking about.

25

A Call to Susan

Dot's conversation with Jim reminds her of Germaine, which makes her think about Susan. If she calls Susan, rather than the other way around, maybe Susan will stop criticizing her. She punches in Susan's number before she can change her mind.

Susan picks up at once. She knows Dot's been ignoring her calls, and she's tempted to let Dot's call go to voicemail, to show her how it feels, but she makes a quick decision to take it, realizing it will put her in the right. "OMG, I can't believe you called!" she says brightly. "Germaine, sweetie, guess who's on the phone!" There's a pause, and then Susan's voice comes on again, echoey. "I'm putting you on speaker."

"No, I can't guess," says Germaine. "You have too many friends."

"Not a friend," says Susan. "Now guess."

"So, a bill collector," says Germaine.

"You're cute," says Susan. "It's Dot! My long-lost sister."

"I'm sorry," says Dot, although she doesn't know what she's apologizing for. It was Susan who got so impatient with Dot's recovery, after all.

"Water under the bridge," says Susan. "Don't even think about it. You'll never guess what's happened! My mortgage has been approved!"

"What," says Dot, "are you talking about?"

"Oh, come on, you remember the condo we saw at Maple Grove—"

"Maple Grave, yeah."

"Well, Germaine and I are buying in!"

"Not 'Germaine and I,'" says Germaine. "You only."

"But *cherie*, we've been all over this," says Susan. "I'll front the money and you can pay me back when you're in better financial shape."

"And how will that happen, if I am stuck in Maple Grave?" says Germaine. "I will lose my students—"

"Grove! Grove!" says Susan. "What is wrong with you people?"

"We do not want to be prematurely *agèd!*" cries Germaine. "I am too young for the Grave!"

"Dotty, I'll have to call you back," says Susan. "I want to share my good news with you, but Germaine and I need to talk. You know how it is. Women, right?"

"Right," says Dot. She had been hoping there had been some sort of misunderstanding, but Germaine was right—Susan is serious. She's moving to Maple Grove with Germaine, whether Germain wants to or not. Meanwhile, Jim's been out for a week because his mom got a traffic ticket. And Viola's totally gentrified. At least the conversation didn't get around to her and Ralfie and their hopeless situation. Hanging up, Dot yells, "I don't know what to do!" This actually makes her feel better.

"What?" Ralfie yells back, from the couch.

"Nothing, nothing, nothing!" Dot stomps into the living room. "Why's all this garbage on the coffee table?" She gathers up the beer cans, the box, a paper bag, and some balled-up napkins.

"A couple of the guys stopped by. Shawn and Nelson. They wanted to cheer me up."

"Jeez. Most people bring flowers."

Ralfie burps and grins.

"You are a ten-year-old!" says Dot.

"I wish," says Ralfie.

26

Ralfie at the Bank

When Ralfie goes to the bank, the financial advisor is a total disappointment, no help whatsoever. "We want to liquidate our savings, invest in an apartment in the South End. Elevator building. Couple of bedrooms," she tells him.

"Hmm," he says. "It doesn't look like you have enough here for that. A condo like that runs what? A mill, mill plus?"

That much? thinks Ralfie. But she pushes on. "Well, yeah, of course we'd sell our current place, take out a mortgage—"

"Let's not get too impulsive, Ms. Santopietro," he says. "Liquidating your savings—there's no guarantee, you know, that property values will continue to rise. You could lose a lot of money. Why don't you mull it over for a while, discuss it with your wife."

Ralfie starts to tell him her relationship is none of his goddamn business but thinks the better of it.

"You'd be taking on quite an obligation, quite a risk, you know." He gives her a big fake smile and holds out his hand. Meeting over.

Ralfie shakes it. Leaves. *And you suck*, she thinks, back out on the sidewalk. *Nobody gets it!* Spend money, make money. Not to mention that she and Dot need a place to live that they can actually get in and out of. He had a nerve, the old moneybags. Although really he looks like a kid. Probably thought he was being helpful, Ralfie mentally concedes. Just out of college, probably wearing the suit his parents bought him for graduation. Nicely tailored, though, with a retro tie he picked out himself, to jazz it up. In the old days, she would have clocked him as one of the tribe, but now? You never know.

She has been giving some thought to Margaret O'Connell. Ralfie was surprised to hear she had retired. Margaret had a wisecrack for anyone who stopped by her desk, and she didn't look anywhere near sixty-five. For decades, she and the girls from the neighborhood had a regular Wednesday poker game. According to Margaret, they hadn't missed a night since the Blizzard of '78, and everyone at the DPW knew when she came out ahead, because she would bring in a couple of boxes of doughnut holes to pass around the office. She herself never ate any. "Not on my diet," she would say.

Maybe it's her health, Ralfie thinks. Margaret was a hopeless smoker, much as she tried to quit every year, on Smoke-Out Day. She would have gotten a break on her medical insurance, but she would admit, "I'm an addict. The girls say, 'Margaret, you can do anything you put your mind to. Look at you and that diet.' But the diet's nothing, compared to the cigs. I try wicked hard, but it doesn't take for more than a couple-three days." Shrugging on a coat or digging out an umbrella, she would trudge outside in all weathers, as if to a wearisome job, to light up.

Back at home, filling out the online employment application, Ralfie realizes she'll miss the old gal. *A good egg*, she thinks. But like the voiceover used to intone in the old movies, as the calendar pages fell away, "Time marches on!" You can't step in the same river twice, they say—although Ralfie could swear she's done just that, dangling her feet off the bank of the filthy Charles one sweltering August afternoon.

Won't it be a pisser if she doesn't get the job, she hopes against hope, as she clicks the "submit" button.

But of course, she does get the job. It even comes with a raise. "If I'd known that before, I would've taken a desk job ages ago," Ralfie tells Nelson. This time he's come without Shawn, and without a six-pack. Instead, he's cutting up a mango.

"Ha! I think not."

"Okay, maybe not. But it's not a bad opportunity, right?"

"Crazy how much I paid for this," he says, handing Ralfie a slice of mango and a napkin. "At home, in my country, they grow on the trees."

"That's how they grow," says Ralfie, "in anyone's country."

"I mean, you can just grab one off a tree, when you're walking down the sidewalk. You don't have to go to no Whole Foods."

"They have sidewalks?"

"Watch your mouth, girl," says Nelson, handing her another piece of mango. "Don't insult my home."

"This is pretty good," says Ralfie. "I never actually ate one before."

"Island specialty. You just have to know how to cut it up."

"You ought to look into something like this job, Nellie. Easy work. Good pay."

"Yeah, right," he says. "Just because you are doing it. You didn't think you were cut out for it before. I'm not either. Not yet."

Ralfie sighs. "Maybe I'll turn it down," she muses.

"Get real, girl! What would your lady think if you did that? She's got a head on her shoulders."

"She wouldn't think anything. I haven't told her about it!"

Nelson shakes his head. "How you can make a decision like that without talking—"

"Hey, gimme another slice," Ralfie interrupts him.

Nelson hands her the last piece of mango and continues. "Me and *my* friend, we don't do nothing without consulting . . ."

Ralfie holds still, as though he has placed in her palm a fragile butterfly instead of a piece of drippy fruit. He never finishes these sentences. Like now, after he offers this advice, he falls silent—yet he knows perfectly well the type of person Ralfie is. For god's sake, she would totally welcome him into the fold. And she would say nothing about it to anyone, not if he didn't want her to. Well, she would tell Dot, that doesn't count, but not the guys—not that they would care. They've been working together for years, everyone's sussed him out. Does he not realize this? "Thanks," she says. "You know, for the mango." She'll never understand him.

"Okay, but you ought to talk—"

"I know, I know," says Ralfie. "I get myself in trouble when I don't . . ." She flashes on the investment counselor, quickly puts him out of her mind.

"That's right," says Nelson. "You got to be honest with each other."

"But it's like the end of an era!" She had gotten excited about the complaint department when she was filling out the paperwork, but now all she can think of is how much she'll miss her old job. The fun of it. The guys. Nelson.

"Maybe for you it is," says Nelson.

"For the truck too! And you guys!"

"Okay, for the truck too." Nelson admits, "I'll miss you. We had some good times." He gathers the mango skins and pit in a napkin and takes them into the kitchen. Returning, he tells Ralfie, "Gotta run." He gives her a quick hug, which surprises her, and leaves.

Running, she thinks morosely. That's over with.

27

They Still Can't Believe

Although Dot and Ralfie still can't believe Susan's really going to move to Maple Grave, they agree to help her pack. But when they arrive, she's sitting on the kitchen floor, surrounded by pots and pans and empty boxes, sobbing.

"Susan, Susan, what happened?" says Dot, immediately folding herself to the floor beside Susan and putting an arm around her shoulder. With her free hand, she finds a tissue in her pocket and passes it to her sister. She's seen her in all kinds of moods and snits but never anything quite like this.

Ralfie, meanwhile, stands awkwardly looking down at them. Sisters, she thinks. She doesn't have one, which is probably why she has no idea what to do. She pulls up a kitchen chair and sits, legs stretched out in front of her, arms crossed, and tries to pretend she can be useful in this situation.

Susan blows her nose. "Germaine," she chokes out.

"Oh no, Susan—is she okay?" says Dot. "Did something happen to her?"

Susan shrugs. "Who knows?"

"Who knows?"

"She's left me. She's not going to help me pack, or move with me to the new apartment, or see me ever again." Susan shakes her head, and her eyes well up. "I keep trying her number, but she won't pick up. She said she wanted a *nouveau depart*. I thought she meant she was going someplace, you know, *departing*, but—"

"At least you won't have to learn any more French," offers Ralfie.

"She wants a clean break. She claims she doesn't want to be tempted to come back to me."

"Oh, Susan," says Dot. "But maybe that means she will. Come back."

"No." Susan sighs. "Not gonna happen. I know her. You might not see her that way, but she can be very determined."

"The little bitch!" says Ralfie before Dot can stop her, because she knows how these things go, and Susan won't want to hear Germaine maligned. Yet. That will come later. "She was probably stepping out on you the whole time!"

"She's not a bitch!" Susan cries. "She's my beautiful *cherie*! And she was *not* having an affair, Ralfie. I would have known."

"That's what they all say," says Ralfie.

"Poor Susan!" says Dot. "My poor little sis."

Susan sniffles, and Dot hands her another tissue. "And I've sold this place, and I have to move—by myself!" Susan honks into the tissue. "Dotty! You know how I felt. I thought this relationship—this was it. The one. You know, like you and Ralfie. I thought we'd have years together."

"You've always been a romantic," says Dot, although she doesn't really believe this. Ralfie is hardly a romantic hero.

"Yes," says Susan, smiling through tears. "I have."

Ralfie rolls her eyes.

"It's true!" Susan insists. "My weakness. I still love her."

Maybe, thinks Dot. And maybe it's all a fantasy in Susan's head. Dot herself never believed Germaine would move to Maple Grave; Germaine as much as told her so. And Germaine was probably trying to tell Susan, too—but as Dot well knows, Susan doesn't always listen to things she doesn't want to hear. Dot didn't believe Susan would move either—but that's definitely the scene right now, whether Susan still wants it or not. "Let's try to do a little packing," Dot suggests. "At least finish the kitchen."

"Right. Let's get this show on the road," says Ralfie, reaching down to grab a nest of saucepans and piling it into a box with the handles sticking out the top.

"Wrap them, wrap them!" says Susan. "They'll get all banged up if you pack them like that!" She stands up and hands Ralfie a roll of bubble wrap from the counter. "And I have plenty of boxes, you don't have to smash all my things into one."

Having someone to instruct is always good for pulling Susan out of a mood, thinks Dot, grateful for Ralfie's impatience.

But Susan starts moaning again. "Oh, fuck it. What's it matter? Mrs. Dailey's probably going to be my new best friend."

A week later, when the moving truck has come and gone, and Susan and her stuff have been deposited at Maple Grave, she is in fact greeted by the indefatigable Mrs. Dailey, who punches at Susan's new doorbell until it buzzes like an angry bee. When Susan finds her way around all the boxes and yanks the door open, there's Mrs. Dailey on the threshold, smiling her vermilion smile and holding out a towering basket of surreal fruit. "It's the welcome wagon lady," she sings out. "Please enjoy this, Susan, gratis. We give one to all our new residents."

Susan gets rid of her and, suddenly ravenous, bites into one of the rosy pears, but it's overripe and mealy, and she hopes its deceptive surface is not a sign of things to come. She tosses the core into the kitchen sink, although she no longer remembers whether Mrs. Dailey's ecstatic recital of the unit's conveniences included a disposal. If not, she thinks, she'll stuff it down the drain anyway. Not her problem. There's a manager to unclog it, and she'll figure out what to do with the rest of the fruit basket tomorrow. Maybe she can have it reposted to Germaine.

28

Asking Viola

Dot wonders whether asking Viola about the apartment violated some sort of relationship boundary that she was not aware of, because since their last lunch, Viola hasn't called, and she hasn't picked up when Dot's called her—not at all typical Viola behavior. When a couple of weeks go by with no word, Dot gets worried. What if Viola is ill? What if she, like Dot, had a heart attack—but with no Ralfie to help her?

She decides to check out the situation in person, and goes over to Viola's building. She pounds on Viola's apartment door and finally, panicking, yells, "Hey! Viola! Anybody home?"

A short, round woman emerges from an apartment across the hall. She is wearing a flowered housecoat and her hair is set with pink sponge curlers, like Dot hasn't seen since high school. She wonders where one buys such things these days.

"What the heck is all that uproar?" the woman demands.

"I'm sorry I disturbed you," Dot says. "I'm looking for my friend."

"Who? Ms. Cottage?"

"Viola, yes."

"Well, if you're such a great friend, you ought to know. She was in the hospital—"

"Oh my god!"

"And rehab. They say she'll be home in a couple of days. We hope. *We,* you know. Her friends."

"But what happened?"

"She fell."

"Fell!"

"Hit her head, so I heard. I don't know the details. We had the ambulance here and everything. Quite a to-do, I can tell you." Shaking her head, which waggles the curlers, she seems annoyed about the ambulance.

"But why didn't she call me?"

"I can't answer that one, Missy—"

"Dot."

"Oh, so you're the famous Dot! Well, Dot, Ms. Cottage has her ways, as I'm sure you know—"

"But which rehab is she in? Where can I find her?"

"I'm not so sure I should give out that information to just anybody who turns up and bangs on her door. She's a very private person."

"But you even said you've heard of me! We're old friends!"

"So you say."

Dot gets the impression that the woman is enjoying her power to exasperate. "But why else would I be here? Viola would want me to know!"

"Maybe," says the woman, retreating back into her apartment. Reassuringly, Dot hears her opening and closing drawers, and muttering to herself, and when she finally reappears, she hands Dot a scrap of paper with a phone number. "Just don't be giving this out to all and sundry," she warns.

"Oh, no," Dot promises, wondering what all-and-sundry the woman thinks would be interested. "Thank you so much, Ms.—what is your name?"

"Hah!" says the woman, "none of your beeswax!" She slams her door.

What a neighbor, Dot thinks, pushing the call button for the elevator. Viola's building is weirder than she realized; she and Ralfie are probably lucky they can't afford it. But she'll think about that later. Mostly, her mind is on the bad news about Viola. She can't understand why Viola didn't contact her. And later, when she calls the number on the paper, Viola is not delighted to hear from her.

"Who gave you this number?" she asks.

"Your neighbor," says Dot.

"Pink curlers?" asks Viola.

"That's the one."

"She hardly ever takes them out."

"That can't be good for her hair," says Dot.

"I don't think she has much anyway," says Viola. "Sometimes she switches them for turquoise. Were you there bothering the manager about a vacancy?"

"No!" says Dot. "You told me. That's impossible. I was worried about you. Why didn't you call me?"

There's a brief silence, and Viola sighs. "I'm sorry, dear. I don't like to burden anyone with these little setbacks."

"Little! But you were in the hospital! You're in rehab! How is that *little*?"

"Oh, come on," says Viola, apparently trying for carelessness. "At my age, it's nothing much. Compared to what *could* happen, I mean. I'll be home in a day or two, and we'll go out to lunch. How's that?"

"It's ridiculous. I don't even know if you're in any condition to go out to lunch."

"I'm surprised Miss Nosy next door didn't tell you the whole story."

"She was into withholding information."

"Ah. That's her other mode. Well, Dotty, it's simple. I was peacefully eating my dinner in front of the TV when that appalling orange person, you know, our so-called president, came on. And I refuse to listen any longer to that man, just brazenly lying to our faces. So I turned off the TV and stood up to clear my plate. And that's when I fainted."

"You fainted! Has that ever happened before?"

Viola hesitates. "Oh, maybe. Once or twice. I was only out for a moment. But I must've cracked my head on the coffee table when I went down, because I bled all over my beautiful Turkish rug. You can still see a stain. I'm quite upset about it."

"I don't care about the rug—"

"The rug is unique! I bought it years ago, on my travels. It has a sentimental value that perhaps you don't understand."

"I'm sorry. But I'm worried about you, not your decor."

"Well, I lay there bleeding for a while, recovering from fainting, you know. Then I realized my phone was on the coffee table, so I crawled over to it and called 911. And of course then you know what happens—all hell breaks loose. The super, the neighbors, the EMTs. A lot of people running around and shouting at each other. At the emergency room, I was admitted to the hospital because they wanted to make sure the fainting wasn't something more serious, and that I hadn't broke any bones.

"But I had," Viola concludes. "Wrist. And I was a bit concussed as well. This never would have happened under Obama."

Dot groans.

"People fracture wrists all the time, Dotty."

Bone breaks are the beginning of the end, thinks Dot.

"Stop that right now!" Viola interrupts. "I know exactly what you're thinking, and it is not true. I'll be out of the cast in a few weeks, and my orthopedist says because I am an otherwise healthy individual, I will recover in short order. The therapists here are excellent—in fact, they are the reason I haven't gone home yet. They can give me better therapy here, with their machines and such."

"I'd like to visit," says Dot.

"No, I don't want anyone to see me, in my condition. You can visit me at home."

"But will you call me when you get out?"

"Humph," says Viola.

"Promise!"

"Oh, all right. But I never realized you could be so interfering."

"You mean, 'I never realized you could be such a good friend, dear Dotty,'" says Dot.

Finally Viola laughs. "You are incorrigible! Okay, hand on my heart. Girl Scout's honor, I will call you the minute I get home. But I want you to understand, I am perfectly able to handle all this myself."

"Understood," says Dot. But she's skeptical. This insistence on total independence and secrecy is a side of Viola she hasn't seen before. Until now she always seemed to welcome a little help—a hand on the elbow when crossing the street, a ride to an evening concert because her night vision has become so poor. So maybe it's something new. A concussion symptom. *Like a two-year-old who insists on tying her own shoes just when her mother is trying to rush her out the door*, Dot thinks, and immediately suppresses the simile. *Don't go there*, she tells herself.

29

Her Breakfast Egg

Dot is serving Ralfie her breakfast egg when Ralfie announces, "So, I won't have to go down to the garage in the morning anymore. I'll be working right here."

Dot stares at her.

Ralfie explains, between bites. "My new job. Complaint desk. You know, flat cat?"

"What are you *talking* about?"

"When the guys were here? With the beer? Shawn said Margaret O'Connell retired."

"Who?"

"Old Margaret," says Ralfie. "Well, she wasn't so old, but she ran the complaint desk. Now that'll be me. Shawn says it'll be fun, people fill out forms, like 'flat cat.' And of course they love me over at the Department, they let me do whatever I want, work from home if I need to."

"You're off the truck," Dot realizes. She was not expecting this, not now. Or maybe ever. "You've got to be kidding me."

"Nope, it's true. From here on, I take it easy."

"But—"

"I changed my mind, okay?"

"I'm in shock. Is this really what you want?"

Ralfie sighs. "It doesn't matter anymore what I want, Dot. You know and I know I can't do that job anymore."

Of course she can't. But for Ralfie to accept the situation and actually do something about it? When the woman lets go of her bravado and comes down to earth, Dot thinks, she sticks her landing. Like the way she's been talking about Viola's building. That caught Dot by surprise. Ralfie's idea about buying an apartment there is completely misguided; it's totally crazy, in Dot's opinion. But maybe she should see it as a good sign, Ralfie coming to terms with her limitations.

"I'm still getting used to the idea," Ralfie admits. "It's a big change."

"I'm not used to the idea at all," Dot agrees. "Change is hard."

"I can take hard. This is different."

"Is that why you didn't tell me until just now?"

"Something like that." Ralfie pauses. "But then Nellie said I had to. He even referred to his *friend!* It was kind of amazing, Dot. You know what he's like—but he came just this close to saying the word." Ralfie holds up a thumb and forefinger a millimeter apart.

"Wow. Then he clammed up, right?"

"He's never going to change, that guy. Not like us, huh? Free and open."

"Ralfie, how could you think you'd start a different job and I wouldn't notice?"

"Especially when you see my big paycheck!" Ralfie tries for her usual enthusiasm. Fails. Dot wouldn't buy it, anyway. "I don't know, I just couldn't deal with having a big talk about what I should do. The leg—it's exhausting. I don't have the energy."

"Yeah, right." What Ralfie has the energy for and what she doesn't. But Dot gets it. Ralfie will miss the strenuous work, the camaraderie with the guys, the variety from day to day. But when you come right down to it, it's the identity. The quintessential butchiness of it. Ralfie was always so proud when someone asked where she worked. And Dot, she was proud too. A prissy librarian waltzing around on the arm of a stone butch. Of course, that's just an image. Dot's about as prissy as Ralfie is stone—in other words, not. "You still are who you are, you know," she says, to reassure them both. "It's nothing to do with the truck."

"*I yam what I yam, and that's all what I yam,*" Ralfie sings. Dot's not going to make a fuss because they didn't have some endless Talk about the new job, she realizes with relief. "Popeye. Remember him? The cartoon?"

"Gloria Gaynor too. '*I am what I am!*'"

"We used to dance to that one. Back when we went to bars. How come we don't do that anymore?"

Not this again, Dot thinks. There are no more bars. And if there are, the women in them are all twenty-one-year-olds who don't believe in labels, or at least not the labels Dot and Ralfie's generation used, and they never heard of Popeye or Gloria Gaynor. "We go to dinner parties with our friends," she says. "And dance in the living room. And you're my favorite butch. Always."

"You know what?" says Ralfie. "You still turn me on."

"But what did you mean about the cat?"

"Shawn said somebody said . . ." Ralfie pushes herself up from the table and hops over to Dot. "Forget the cat. Give us a hug."

30

Unresolvable Life Crises

Ralfie, Viola, Susan—even Jim the intern. Everyone Dot knows is in the midst of some essentially unresolvable life crisis. And Dot herself? She feels spun around, like a child on a swing set pushed off center, entangled in the ropes and twisting in circles. Swings have been deemed too dangerous by some and removed from the playgrounds. And all this is giving her a headache. Spinning around is for kids.

At least she can visit Viola, who's home from rehab and back in communication. She's been sounding so lonely and bored. "Because I'm stuck in here all day," she told Dot, who's of course heard this kind of thing before, from Ralfie. "Exercises, television, even reading, which as you know I've always loved—without some human contact, it's not enough for the vigorous mind."

"What about your neighbor? Isn't she around?"

"Her? Oh, please."

So Dot promised. "I'll be over this weekend."

"Lucky girl," Viola said. "With a job you can go to. My days are all the same. A weekend means nothing anymore."

Dot's a little surprised, when she enters the apartment, at the disarray. Viola can't keep the place up to her usual standard of orderliness—Dot understands that—but there are dirty dishes on the coffee table and a half-eaten container of unidentifiable takeout on the kitchen counter. The bed is unmade. And Viola herself, sitting in a big armchair in the living room with her bad arm immobilized in a huge cast and propped on a pillow, is wearing a stained sweater and has not combed her hair.

"So good to see you, my dear!" Viola greets her. "Tell me all the gossip!"

"You first," says Dot. "How are you managing?"

"Well, I'm off the heavier painkillers, which just left me nauseated, and on some combination of ibuprofen and Tylenol. I'm not really sure which is which, but the girl sets it up for me."

"The home health aide? Isn't she also supposed to help with the dishes and things?"

"Yes, of course. A lovely girl. Very patient, I must say, since I'm quite aware that I can be demanding."

"Then why . . ." Viola doesn't seem to have noticed the condition of her apartment, so Dot stops herself.

"What?"

"Nothing. I think I'll tidy up a bit." Dot stands and collects the dishes.

"Put those down! I told you, the girl will fix it. She's just a little late today."

"She doesn't seem very competent," says Dot. "I mean, I'm sure she's nice and everything . . ."

Viola's face reddens. She looks down and with her good arm brushes ineffectually at the stain on her sweater. "I'm a mess, aren't I."

"It's not like you."

"I hate this. I know I need the help, but I hate it. I refuse!"

"I don't understand—"

"There is no girl," Viola confesses. "I made that up."

"Oh, for chrissake!" says Dot. Maybe the problem is that everyone—everyone in the world!—is secretly insane. "You admitted it yourself, you're not managing—"

"Dot, really! Stop. I won't hear of it. When I'm better, I'll give everything a good hard scrubbing. You can come over and help me."

"Gee, thanks," says Dot. "Look, I don't agree with you. You need help—someone who comes in regularly to make sure you're taking the right meds, keeping up with your exercises, cleaning, shopping. Why is that so terrible?"

"It just is," says Viola. "A stranger in my house, touching my things."

"But they wouldn't be a stranger once you got to know them! Like the girl—you said she was lovely and patient."

"She's imaginary! If you don't understand, Dotty, I cannot explain it to you."

They leave it there, Dot shaking her head. Viola chatters on about her adorable physical therapist, who she is sure is gay—but Dot isn't paying much attention. Her mind is still on the alleged aide. When it's her turn to say something, she comments automatically, "All PTs are gay."

"No, you're confused. That's sign-language interpreters. Look at Ralfie's Shelly. Straight as a cheerleader."

"Gay," says Dot. "Cheerleaders too. Ralfie says Shelly just doesn't know it yet."

31

A Cold, Rainy Sunday

It's a cold, rainy Sunday. Ralfie's fallen asleep on the couch after an afternoon of football watching. Dot is fretting about dinner—since if Ralfie has made any plans, she hasn't told Dot about them—when Susan unexpectedly appears at the door with a shopping bag full of takeout. Thai, Dot concludes, from the scent of fish sauce.

"Oh, thank goodness—I had no idea what to do about supper," Dot welcomes her.

"How about, 'Hello, dear sister, how are you doing in that isolated hellhole you live in?' Am I nothing to you but a delivery service?"

Dot leans over the shopping bag and gives Susan a kiss. "Oh, Susan, stop. You know I'm glad to see you."

"I do?" asks Susan. "Then why don't you ever come up to my new place?"

"Traffic?" says Dot. It's actually true. She herself has cultivated a Zen-like attitude toward the city's inexplicable tie-ups, but Ralfie's never learned. After miles of stop-and-go, when they're suddenly zooming along, and there's no apparent reason for either the slow-down or the flow, Ralfie starts cursing the other drivers, giving them the finger and making other obscene gestures, some of which she seems to have invented. Dot's composure breaks down. A road trip often leaves them both frazzled and annoyed with each other.

"It's bad," Susan agrees. "Especially this afternoon. But that's no excuse. Traffic is everywhere."

"Weren't we supposed to get flying cars?" muses Dot, taking the shopping bag from Susan, who follows her into the kitchen. Dot unloads the takeout containers onto the kitchen counter. "Like in science fiction. Do you think we should warm these in the microwave?"

"We can do that later, if you don't want to eat right away. And that was just the Jetsons. Hardly quality sci-fi."

"Let's wait until Ralfie wakes up. That will give us a chance to talk. How is Maple—"

"*Grove*," Susan preempts her.

"Okay, *Grove*. Groove. Maple Groovy. How's it going?"

Susan sighs. "You guys are incorrigible. I know you think I've made a huge mistake—"

"No, no," Dot lies.

"But actually, it's getting better. At first Mrs. Dailey kept coming around. You know, every couple of days, to see how I was settling in. I think she's lonely. But I had to shake her off. No one else would talk to me because they thought I was friends with her. Cynthia—the concierge, remember?"

"The one behind the flower arrangement?"

"She clued me in. She *hates* Mrs. Dailey! Because of the way Dailey constantly mangles her name—like Cyn-thi-a's not worth three full syllables. But anyway, Cynthia is adorable—really sweet, friendly. A truly *good person*, you can just tell. And you saw how attractive she is. I always seem to go for those dark-haired types—"

"Susan, I've heard this before. Anyway, Cynthia dyes her hair blonde."

"That's just a look—"

"I hope it works out this time. For the two of you."

"Nothing's happened! She could be married, for all I know." Susan leans in to Dot and says confidentially, "Actually, I asked her out. We're going next week. To the Red Rooster—she says it's her favorite."

Like a character in a Saturday morning cartoon—the Jetsons, perhaps—Ralfie levitates in on the smell of food as it curls in wisps from the containers on the counter. "Mmmm," she hums. Sitting down and opening a few containers, she corrects Susan. "Lobster! Not Rooster. Now that you're in Maple—"

"*Grove*," Susan interrupts.

"Whatever. The restaurant is called Red Lobster."

"Ralfie, I should think I know what Cynthia said. She said 'rooster.'"

Ralfie shrugs. "You'll see. It'll be all straight-date-night-in-the-burbs."

"It's not a date."

"It's not?" says Dot. "But a minute ago, you said it was."

"Well, I'm not sure if it is or it isn't," Susan admits. "I can't exactly tell what Cynthia thinks of it."

"In that case, it's definitely a date!" says Dot.

"Dot's right," agrees Ralfie. "If you don't know if it's a date, you're dating a lesbian. Who would've thought, up there in the old-age home."

Ignoring Ralfie, Susan tells Dot, "I think the rules are different in Maple Grove."

"They're universal," says Dot. "Promise you'll call right after and tell me all about it."

As it turns out, Susan is right. It's the Rooster, and it's gay. The only surviving lesbian bar in New England, and it's in an obscure strip mall next to a closed dog-wash business. But there's lots of parking, and inside, the lights are low, the bar is well stocked, and the booths are cozy. "There's dancing downstairs," Cynthia points out, although she doesn't have to. Susan can feel the thud of the bass beneath her feet. "And the food up here is really good. They got a new cook last year, and she revamped the menu and toned down the lighting. We even got cloth napkins and table service."

So maybe it *is* a date. "Ralfie thought you were taking me to a Red Lobster. You know, Mr. Belrose?"

"Ha!" says Cynthia. "That was a good one. Mrs. Dailey still doesn't know what hit her."

Cynthia orders a chicken caesar and a glass of white wine, so Susan does too, although she was considering the Giant Rooster Cheesy Burger with Genuine Lower East Side Kosher Pickle and Fries, until Cynthia explained that she is trying to cut down on red meat. So, Susan thinks disappointedly, the Rooster Burger might offend.

Conversation is awkward, each promising start fading away as Cynthia deflects questions about her family and living situation. Susan has never heard of most of Cynthia's favorite TV shows, and their tastes in music overlap only in the case of Celine Dion's "My Heart Will Go On," which Susan would never admit, to anyone, and anyway it's only because the song brings her back to a certain slow dance with Germaine. They receive dessert menus.

"You have to try this one—chocolate lava bombe. With ice cream. And whipped cream. It's their specialty," Cynthia says, her eyes shining.

It's just a dessert, thinks Susan, who usually passes on sweets, although she did go through that period of trying to tempt Dot with them. *No need to get all excited*. But she and Cynthia are both still hungry, having had only salad for dinner. "Ice cream *and* whipped cream?" she says. "Isn't that going a little overboard?"

"Oh, no," says Cynthia. "You need them. To cut the chocolate." And before Susan can intervene, Cynthia orders a bombe with two spoons, and two espressos. "You need those too," she explains. "Trust me. It's the best."

And she turns out to be right. Not so much because of the bombe, which in Susan's opinion is more chocolate than anyone really needs, but because as they dip their spoons into the cream, their eyes meet, the evening's awkwardness falls away, and Susan feels an unexpected flash of— understanding? Connection? Desire. Her clit pings. Cynthia smiles at her, as though she knows exactly what's going on, and Susan smiles back.

"Now for the espresso," says Cynthia. She raises the little cup, downs it in a swallow, and smacks it back onto the table. "Your turn."

Susan follows. The coffee is hot and bitter, astringent. She doesn't usually take it black.

The evening's awkwardness returns as they negotiate the check and gather their things to leave, but in the parking lot, Cynthia thanks Susan for a great evening, pulls her close, and smooches her right on the lips. She jumps into her car and speeds off, her hand waving out the window.

"So," Susan asks Dot afterward, on the phone. "Date or no date?"

"I think you'll have to ask her out again to figure it out."

"She's probably just shy," says Susan.

32

A Few Stray Magenta Highlights

Jim reappears at work with a new haircut—a neat brush, with a few stray magenta highlights. "I like it," says Dot.

"*I* liked the colors. But my mom acted like they were an even worse tragedy than the traffic ticket. I couldn't stand feeling so bad for her."

"So, problems solved?" says Dot. "Everything peaceful?"

Jim closes his eyes and shakes his head. "Only the hair. I thought I told you, my mom quit work, and she refuses to go out. And meanwhile my dad says, 'You stay in school. Learn. Get a good job.' So they won't take my help, but they can't make it on just his income. I mean, he's a smart guy, but his education's basically worthless here, so he's a janitor at the hospital where she was a nurse's aide—"

"Wait. Your mother was a nurse's aide?"

"She's a trained nurse! She's very emphatic about that. But in this country? Her boss, and the other nurses—they all love her. Her boss even said she wished she could promote her. But will my mom ask for her old job back? No way! She goes, 'No more W-4 tax form! From now on, only under the bench!'" He laughs. "She doesn't always get the idioms right. Stubborn old thing."

Her and everyone else, thinks Dot. Why do they all refuse the most obvious, reasonable course of action? At least Ralfie finally got herself off the truck. But look at Susan! Thinking she'll find love out in the suburbs. Look at Viola! "Viola," she says.

"Viola?" says Jim.

"My friend," says Dot, thinking through the arrangement in her head. "I think your mom could help her. Under the table." The pieces ought to fit together easily. Dot sighs. "Although she's pretty stubborn, too."

"I still don't understand . . ."

"My friend Viola, she's in her eighties, she fell and got a concussion and broke her wrist, and now she's a mess, she has no idea what pills she's taking, she's depressed—"

"My mom says geriatric patients are often the most difficult."

"But she says she refuses to have a stranger in her apartment. Maybe if we introduced your mom as a friend, someone I want Viola to meet . . . ," Dot muses.

"My mom won't go for that," says Jim. "My parents don't really know anyone who's not Vietnamese. And she wouldn't trust a white person not to turn her into Immigration. Is Viola Vietnamese?"

"Of course not!"

"Why 'of course'? Is it so unlikely that you'd have a Vietnamese friend? You have me."

It's nice that Jim considers her a friend, thinks Dot, but as gently as he makes his point, she feels humiliated. The idea of Jim's parents always seems to evoke stereotypes she didn't even know she had. "Well, for one thing, who ever heard of a Vietnamese person named Viola?" she asks defensively.

"Do you think my parents named me Jim? My original name was Binh." That, combined with his short stature, caused him endless trouble in the schoolyard. His parents couldn't understand it. "It's a beautiful name. Means peaceful."

"Americans think it's funny," he had tried to explain. "The kids call me Garbage Bin."

"How do they think of things like that? You must ignore them," his parents had told him. "Be strong." But once again, they had realized, this country isn't all it's cracked up to be.

By age ten, he had had more than enough. Outside his home, he began to call himself Jim. Jim Tran. Simple, masculine monosyllables. His parents were hurt that he had rejected the name they had given him. It was a long time before they learned to pronounce the new one. "I'd change it back, but it's too late, now that I've convinced everyone to call me Jim. Even my parents. Even me. I probably wouldn't answer to my real name. Binh. Who's he?"

"Well, Viola is a total Yankee. Ancestor on the Mayflower, teacups inherited from her great-grandmother. Daughters named Viola going back to the 1800s."

"Forget it, then," says Jim. "My mom would never believe Viola wants to meet her. Anyway, if Viola doesn't want a caregiver, then my mom can't do much for her, right?"

Dot pulls on her hair in frustration, and her bun unravels. Rewinding it, she stabs it through with a pencil she grabs from her desk. People are so annoying. Her solution would benefit everyone! Viola, Jim's mother, Jim—even Dot herself, since she could stop worrying about the takeout containers on Viola's kitchen counter and whether or not Jim would show up on any given day. "Well, all I can say is, this whole situation *sucks*," she concludes, Ralfie-like.

33

A Favor for Jim's Mom

"What's the big problem?" says Ralfie. "Just tell Viola she'd be doing Jim's mom a favor."

"But why would she want to do a favor for Jim's mom?" says Dot.

"A favor to you, then. You're Jim's boss. Put it that way. Plus, she'd be helping out a poor immigrant."

"Jim's mom has a green card. She's practically a citizen."

"Viola doesn't have to know that."

"I can't think about this anymore," says Dot, although Viola's situation has been obsessing her, like a tune she can't get out of her head. What they call an earworm. Horrible image. To rid herself of the obsession, she's tried hopping up and down, shaking her head to one side then the other, like you would do after swimming, to get the water out of your ears. She's yawned until her jaw cracks. No pop. She dropped in again on Viola and caught herself noticing two more spots on Viola's blouse. She's counting them, for god's sake. "How was work today?"

"Not bad," says Ralfie.

In fact, she's digging this job. Most of the complaints she logs are routine — a pothole, a broken streetlight, an electrical short that plunges an entire neighborhood into darkness. But at least once a day, something interesting comes up. Shawn was right. And it's not only flat cats. For example, graffiti. It's amazing what people write, and where they write it. The latest: a landlord from Dorchester who called, livid, because someone spray-painted the side of his brick six-flat: "I LOVE FAT FEM DYKES."

"I can get behind that," said Ralfie.

"What?" he yelled, outraged. "What'd you say?"

"Nothing," said Ralfie. "Keep your shirt on." All business, she continued, "Spell your name for me, please? Address, phone number. Address of the vandalized surface." She added a few questions of her own. "What color is the slogan?"

"Who cares what color it is? It's obscene! I run a nice building, this is a family neighborhood."

"I have to fill in this form, sir. Just answer the questions. There are many types of families."

The man growled. "Not here! It's purple, okay? Very bright, three-foot-high. Purple. You can't miss it. Asshole must've had an extension ladder."

"And the spelling? Is it spelled correctly?"

"You've gotta be kidding! F-E-M—how the fuck should I know?"

"You don't need to use that kind of language. I'm just trying to help," said Ralfie. "We'll send over a cleanup team. Unless you want us to fix it, tone it down a bit, maybe redo it in gray—"

"Are you out of your mind?"

"If the tag is not gone within fourteen days, you can give us another call."

"I want it done now! Today!"

"You and everybody else, sir," said Ralfie. "We all have to wait our turn in this world." She hung up on him, called Nelson. Knowing the routines, she's been dispatching crews quite efficiently, and she's already gotten a compliment from her boss—who doesn't yet know about her love of improvisation. "Hey, Nellie, we got a graffiti emergency out in Dorchester, maybe you can take care of it today? Or tomorrow?"

"What's it say?" asked Nelson. Ralfie told him, and he laughed. She knew he would appreciate it. One of these days, he'll out himself. "I guess I know some sisters, they could get behind that," he said.

"Just what I told the guy," said Ralfie. "But he didn't take to it."

"We can't do it today, my friend, too much on the schedule already. Tomorrow maybe. But it'll just come back, you know. And the brick won't take the anti-graffiti paint."

"Exactly what I was hoping," said Ralfie.

34

Susan Tries Again

At Dot's suggestion, Susan decides to try again with Cynthia. It would shock Dot, if she knew—Susan taking her advice, or anyone's. Although maybe it's not that Susan is taking Dot's advice, exactly, but rather that she's following her own inclination, which happens to align with Dot's take on the situation. Cynthia has continued to greet Susan warmly from behind the flower arrangement, and Susan takes this as encouragement.

As the encouragement it is meant to be, in fact—and Cynthia is pleased to get another invitation. "Rooster again?" she suggests.

"Nice place," says Susan. "Sure. This time let's check out the dance floor."

"You're on," says Cynthia.

The way Cynthia says this, it sounds like a dare, although Susan isn't sure why that should be. Dancing is dancing. A little hopping up and down, a little twitching of the hips, and finally, when a slow number comes on, Susan likes to pull her partner toward her, place a hand on her waist and an arm around her shoulders, in the classic pose. They dip and slide across the floor, and by the end of the song, Susan has the two of them thoroughly entwined, their hips moving in sync, and Susan whispers into her partner's ear, so softly that the woman is not entirely sure she hears correctly, *"Come home with me."* Susan's forwardness is so unexpected, her authority so appealing—with its promise that as responsible and reliable as you are, you can finally lay your burdens down—that, oh, eighty percent of the time it works. According to Susan's estimate. Her dance partner follows her home in her car and does not change her mind and bolt. She stays the night. After they share a pleasant enough morning coffee, Susan doesn't always call again, but with Cynthia, she thinks, she might. She definitely might.

So much, Susan thinks, for Dot and Ralfie and their taunts. Maple Grove. During Susan's new, long commute, she listens to audiobooks of nineteenth-century novels, since she figures there are enough of them, and they're long enough, to last the rest of her working life. She just has to avoid the more obscure, soporific ones. *Daniel Deronda* nearly got her killed. Between her jobs and her pursuit of Cynthia, she is keeping busy and developing a new social life, after the Germaine disappointment. So much for Germaine. When Susan gets home, she relaxes in front of her new gas fireplace. Things could be worse.

This time, when Cynthia appears, she is wearing a black leather vest over a black T-shirt. Black jeans, black sneakers.

"You look—different," says Susan, unsure of what to make of this new version of the concierge.

"My dancing outfit," says Cynthia.

"I wish I'd known," says Susan. "I'm overdressed." Thinking to impress with her sophistication, she had put on a skirt, a blazer, knee-high boots.

"No way! It suits you. Great boots."

They descend the stairs to the dance floor. The place is literally a dive, a basement lit by strings of Christmas-tree bulbs edging a dropped ceiling and a flashing neon sign in the shape of some sort of poultry hanging behind the bar. "They inherited it from a chicken shack that closed," Cynthia explains. "But nobody would come to a bar called the Pink Chicken. So they decided it's a rooster—I mean, who can tell? That's how the place got its name."

"Actually, 'pink chicken' sounds kind of intriguing," shouts Susan. The sound system seems to be trying to compensate with volume for its poor quality. Over the music, Susan hears people yelling, "Sin! Sin!"

"My buds," says Cynthia, apologetically. "They think it's funny. Honestly, I didn't know they'd be here tonight. But if we don't say hello, they'll be insulted."

"I thought you didn't like nicknames."

"Not Cindy, and not from Mrs. Dailey," says Cynthia. "Nobody calls her by her first name, you know. I don't think she has one." Cynthia pushes through the crowded bar, Susan following in her wake. Somehow Cynthia seems to have taken charge of the evening, although that's normally Susan's role, and Susan is not sure how she feels about this. They stop at a table occupied by two hearty women with identical bowl haircuts—one blonde, one brunette—half-full beer bottles and several empties in front of them.

Their broad bodies match too, and their plaid shirts complement each other: Black Watch, Royal Stewart.

They wave their bottles at Cynthia, and the blonde—Black Watch—says, "We didn't know if you'd show, so we started without you. Now you gotta catch up—at least with Maggy here. I'm only having a couple. Driving."

"I'll never keep up with you guys," says Cynthia. "Lord knows I've tried."

"Ha!" exclaims Maggy. "That you have. Remember that night, Shirl—"

"You remember it?" says Shirl. "I don't think so."

"Unforgettable," says Maggy. She looks Susan up and down, then stretches her arm across the table and lays her head on it, as though to see better from that angle. Lifting her forearm, she points at Susan, sweeping a bottle onto the floor in the process. "Who's the new chick, Sinful?"

Shirl stops the bottle with her foot, leans down with a groan, and grabs it. "Chrissakes, Mags, watch it! Somebody could trip over that thing and kill themselves."

"Not my fault," says Maggy, from the table. "It's a *Rolling* Rock! Get it?"

"No," says Shirl.

"I met her at work. She's living in the old-age home. Can you believe it?" says Cynthia. "Last week she took me to dinner upstairs."

"Oh, *upstairs*," says Maggy. "Hoo hoo."

"What's a cute young thing like her doing in the old-age home?" Shirl asks.

"It's not—" Susan interrupts this discussion of her attributes.

"Okay, *independent living*," says Cynthia. "Call it whatever, but—"

"Then what do you think I'm doing there?" says Susan, starting to feel insulted.

"Beats me," says Cynthia, grabbing the seat of Susan's chair with two hands and pulling it closer to her. "But you're not like the others, are you, babe."

Maggy stands, drains her bottle, and bangs it down on the table. "Next round's on me." Looking down at Susan, she says, "What's your pleasure, New Chick? Beer or beer?"

"I guess beer," says Susan.

"Good choice!" yells Shirl and gives Maggy a fist-bump. "Nothing for me, darlin'."

Susan tries to hand a few bills to Maggy, who waves them away.

"Tradition," says Maggy, squeezing her way around the table. "Newbies get a freebie. Later we'll drink you out of house and home."

Cynthia leans into Susan. "She's good people, really, even if she seems a little crazy. They both are—"

"Rude, Sinful!" Shirl interrupts her. "You never introduced us! What's New Chick's name?"

"My dear! How could I commit such a grievous transgression of proper etiquette?" says Cynthia. "Will you ever forgive me, Mistress Shirley?" She stands and bobs toward Shirl, lifting the hem of an imaginary skirt in a curtsey. "Let me present the honorable Ms. Susan—"

"Greenbaum," says Susan, not sure if Cynthia knows her full name. "Susan Greenbaum."

"Ms. Susan Greenbaum," announces Cynthia. "Also known, to less intimate acquaintances, as Cyn's New Chick." Turning to Susan, Cynthia says, "May I have this dance?"

"Why, I believe I have a space right here on my dance card, Ms. Cynthia," says Susan, enjoying this game. After the audiobooks, she's well prepared for a little Victorian cosplay. "You surely may." Susan takes Cynthia's hand to lead her to the dance floor as Cynthia looks back at Shirl and grins.

Susan shows off her moves. She likes to do a thing where, leaning back, she twists lower and lower before her partner, then springs up, takes her by the shoulders, twirls her around, and gets the two of them bumping, crotch to ass. It's a little hard on the knees, but Susan figures she still has a few more years of it in her, and Cynthia seems to be appreciating her athleticism. It's when "Sexual Healing" comes on that the problems begin. The dance starts to feel like a tug of war—Susan in her high boots and Cynthia in her leather vest both trying to steer the two of them around the floor. Cynthia stops short. "It's hard for you to let go, I get it," she says. "So listen. I've got this one, but you can have the next."

"Why do *you* get this one?" says Susan.

"Mmm, maybe I want to see you struggle a little." She pulls Susan closer to her and chants along with Marvin Gaye, *"Come on come on come on come on."*

That's my line, thinks Susan.

This date is not unfolding as she thought it would. But she lets it happen.

35

Alone and Confused

Susan wakes the next morning, alone and confused—although not because she's in an unfamiliar place (she's in her own apartment), and not even because of the rounds of drinks she ended up buying Maggy and Shirl, although there are a few moments from the night, she has to admit, that get a little fuzzy around the edges. Somehow it was Cynthia who took the wheel and drove Susan home to Maple Grove, and Susan never did get her turn to lead, not the dancing and not the sex. It was Cynthia who led once again, right to Susan's bed. That's what's so confusing. The dancing and the sex were dreamy, even though it was only their second date, and they hadn't yet figured out much about one another's desires and quirks. Cynthia intuited, thinks Susan, rolling from her side onto her back and giving her damp pubic hair a friendly pat. Cynthia is an outstanding intuiter. She must have tiptoed out while Susan was still sleeping and gone to her post at the front desk. Susan wonders if she's wearing her leather vest.

Of course she's not wearing her leather vest. She keeps an outfit of Cynthia-appropriate work clothes in a file drawer, although she doesn't need to pull them out as often as Susan might assume. Cynthia's not sure if it was Shirl and Maggy egging her on, gratified to see her dating someone reasonable for once, or Susan's own manifold attractions, as Cynthia sees her, but she hadn't planned on the evening ending quite as it did. She had thought her wild-thing days were over—but fortunately, at least in this case, she still has it in her. Cynthia smiles to herself, just as Mrs. Dailey is walking by. "Why good morning, Sandy—uh—Cindy! How nice to see you looking so cheerful for a change."

"Lovely day!" says Cynthia.

"A little gray—"

"But mustn't we be grateful for every day!" says Cynthia. "Gray or . . . pink!"

"Pink?"

"Like a chicken," says Cynthia. "Especially here in the rest home, where so many of our seniors face illness and dea—"

"Never say that word!" Mrs. Dailey cuts her off. "And do not call this facility a rest home—my goodness! It is adult living. For adults—not *seniors*. Terrible word. Are you and I *juniors*?"

"I don't think you have to worry about that, Mrs. Dailey," says Cynthia, as sweetly as she can manage.

Mrs. Dailey looks at her suspiciously, and Cynthia bats her eyes and smiles.

Someday, mutters Mrs. Dailey, walking away, I'm going to fire that bitch's ass.

36

Distressing Visits

Dot's weekly visits to Viola have become increasingly distressing, as each time Viola's hair looks stringier, her blouses spottier, the kitchen grimmer. Finally, one Saturday, as Dot walks through the door, Viola says, as though continuing a conversation, "I give in. I can't keep living this way. Send in the clowns."

"Clowns?" Dot worries. Old people get urinary tract infections, fevers, delirium.

"It's a song," says Viola, waving away Dot's concern. "I'm fine. Except for the mess around here. You know, my dear, at some point we're not going to be able to take care of ourselves. And we're not heterosexuals. We can't count on our children trying to work out their guilt for all the trouble they caused as adolescents. We have to do for each other. Or find someone . . ."

This cannot get any more exasperating, thinks Dot. "As I've been saying all along—"

Viola ignores her and continues. "So about the home assistants, or whatever you call them. I need a girl."

Dot laughs. "That sounds like something Ralfie would've said in her bar-fly days."

"It's not funny, and don't bring Ralfie into this."

"I'm sorry—"

"I had my moments," says Viola. "My conquests. I was in great demand in my day. Maybe you didn't know me then—"

"How can you say that?" says Dot. This is the kind of statement that makes Dot worry about Viola's mental acuity. "I was one of them," she reminds Viola. "Your conquests."

"Yes, yes," says Viola vaguely, averting her eyes from Dot's concerned look. "You were a delectable young thing."

Dot flashes on the weight bearing down on her chest, the hospital, the beeping monitors and needle sticks. After all that, it's hard to feel delectable. She pulls herself back to the present, where Viola has given her the opening she's been wishing for. And she has the solution to everything! Well, except for her own problems, like the three flights of stairs to her and Ralfie's apartment. But they won't kill her. Not right away. "Viola," she says. "I know exactly what to do."

"Tell!"

"Jim's mom. Jim's our graduate student this year. His mother's a nurse, well, in this country she's been working as an aide, but she lost her job, and she's looking for another, especially if she can be paid off the books."

But Viola looks disappointed. "She doesn't sound very impressive. Why did she lose her job, if she's so skilled? What's this about *off the books*? I'm not opening my home to criminals!"

"Mrs. Tran is not a criminal! She's very experienced and kind." At least, Dot hopes she is, as she realizes that the only thing Jim has said about his mother's character is that she is stubborn. "So she made a right on red. She freaked out when she got the ticket, and she was afraid to leave the house because of the immigration police. So she didn't exactly *lose* her job, she quit—"

Viola shakes her head. "All that sounds extremely suspicious. Why would she get so upset if she wasn't guilty of something? Everybody gets those tickets. The signs are covered by trees, or they've gotten knocked down in car crashes—"

"I know, Ralfie's crew used to have to fix them all the time."

"Ralfie must've been pulling your leg," says Viola. "I've never known one to be fixed. And this Mrs. Tran sounds like a bad business."

"She is not! She's perfect. I think you just can't accept help."

"Now that's absurd! I'm the one who brought it up in the first place."

"Oh, really?" says Dot, who remembers their conversations quite differently.

"I wish I could explain it to you," says Viola, pulling back from the argument. "This is not my life—illness, confinement, aides. I'm *me* on the inside, but on the outside, my body, what it's doing—it's as though it's someone else. Nothing to do with *me*. Do you see, sweetheart?" Her eyes fill. "Or perhaps I'm going insane."

Dot stands and leans over Viola's chair, gives her an intense, awkward hug, takes her hand, and sits back down. They sit together like this for a moment, quietly, each with her own thoughts. "You are not insane," Dot says suddenly.

"Thank you," says Viola, not sarcastically but quite seriously.

Although Dot does not understand the disembodied feeling that Viola describes. Or more accurately, she doesn't want to. The weight on her chest, her depression afterward—her memories of that time are disturbingly muddled. *I will not succumb*, she tells herself, and pats Viola's hand. "How about this? Jim brings his mother for you to interview, and I'm here—"

"And?"

"And," Dot continues, trying to think of something to say that will lighten the atmosphere, "if he and his mom turn out to be criminals, you won't be alone with them, and I'll kick them out of the house!"

"Kick them? I had no idea you could be so violent—"

"Viola! Either you're claiming that this perfectly nice person is dangerous, or you're protecting her. Which is it?"

"Neither, all right?" Viola closes her eyes, waves her hand at Dot in dismissal. "This is all too much right now. Do what you want."

"I will," says Dot stubbornly, as she plans her next steps.

37

Jim Is Wary

Dot calls Jim immediately when she gets home, before Viola can change her mind, but he turns out to be as wary of the arrangement as Viola is. "I told you," he says. "My mom won't feel safe with a white lady. She's worried enough about the immigration police already. She's looking for work in our community. There's plenty of old people who could use the help, but so far no one can afford to pay her."

"That's what I mean! Viola can pay. A lot. At least put your mom on the phone?"

"Dot, no. She doesn't like to talk on the phone. Let me and my dad talk to her first. I think that'll work better."

Ralfie has turned the dining room into her office, with her laptop on the table in front of her, and various binders and handbooks and notepads in piles all around. Dot stomps in, fuming. "I have to tell you this!"

Shaking her head at Dot and pointing at the phone at her ear, Ralfie says, "Yup! First thing tomorrow morning! How did your street get that many potholes, anyway? I mean, even for around here it's a little abnormal—"

"Why are you doing that now?" Dot interrupts.

"The guy next door *dug* them? To slow down the traffic? How come you all didn't just put up a few traffic cones and apply to the city for a speed bump?"

"Ralfie!"

She turns to Dot. "No, shhh," she says, pecking with two fingers at the computer keyboard. "Let me log this call. The guy must be a behemoth, with his own private jackhammer. I bet he smashes up the street again as soon as we finish with it."

"Oh, forget it," says Dot, stomping back out. "You'd think you could let it go to voicemail at this hour!"

"Our Complaint Department never closes," Ralfie calls after her proudly.

"Give me a break!" Dot yells back. It's great that Ralfie has adjusted so well to her new job, but it's taking over their entire apartment—in fact, their entire lives. It's like an addiction. Ralfie never wants to go anywhere anymore, even with Dot, in case she misses a call while they're out. "And what do you mean, *our* and *department*? Is there some other staff around here that I haven't met?"

"I like the sound of it. Gives the city a better image, more invested in customer service, you know? Like they tell you in B-school—it's all about the brand. Sometimes that stuff comes in handy."

"For your information, constituents aren't *customers*. Not everything's buy and sell."

"Whatever," says Ralfie as her phone buzzes again.

Discouraged, Dot figures that when Jim calls back, he'll tell her, again, that white people can't be trusted. He's right, of course. But maybe this once. But there's always *this once*. Everyone thinks they're an exception. But, thinks Dot, she *is* an exception, Viola too. Neither would call the immigration police, not on somebody's mother! Not on Jim's mother, of all people.

Anyway, Dot wouldn't know where to begin, who these immigration police are, exactly. CIA? Because it's international? But how would you call the CIA? She doubts that a vast spy agency has a main switchboard. And if it does, it's probably one of those with a HAL-like computer—2020 update, female—that pretends to want to help you by telling you to punch in various codes, which you never seem to do to its satisfaction, and meanwhile it's downloading your voiceprint or something. And then just for the fun of it, it tells you to hold and your call will be answered in the order it was received, and transfixed into obedience, you do what it says, and it puts on a staticky version of the Winter movement of Vivaldi's Four Seasons that sounds like it was recorded by a not-very-accomplished junior high school orchestra, and when that lovely piece is ruined for you forever, you hang up. Dot's wise to that by now.

Later that night, her phone rings. "Ms. Greenbaum? This is Mr. Bao Tran, Jim's dad. Jim told me and Mrs. Tran about your sick friend. We are very sorry."

"Thanks," says Dot, thinking, *he's turning me down*. She tries to explain. "Viola, my friend, is not sick, exactly. But she can't take care of herself. She fell and banged herself up, and she has a broken wrist." Dot hesitates, then admits, "Sometimes she gets confused, too. In my opinion. She knows she needs help, but she also doesn't want it. Do you know what I mean? She is very stubborn."

"Ha ha!" exclaims Mr. Tran. "Mrs. Tran can best her in that arena!"

"I don't know about that—"

"Oh, yes, my wife is like a dog with a bone!" he says proudly. "Ms. Greenbaum—"

"Dot."

"Dot, okay. Dot, our family has discussed this job. I am calling on behalf of Mrs. Tran. She does not like to talk on the phone—she is self-conscious, her accent, you understand. Mrs. Tran says she will help out your friend. But she is very expensive. She is a *trained nurse.*"

"Viola will appreciate that," Dot reassures him. "When they meet, they can work out the details."

"But Mrs. Tran will not sign any papers. Absolutely not."

"No problem!" says Dot.

"And no checks. Cash only!"

"No problem," Dot repeats, realizing this could create some logistical issues. Maybe Mrs. Tran could do the bank run herself. Better, Dot could send Ralfie, which would separate her from the Complaint Department. Or, best idea yet—she and Ralfie could drive to the bank together! On the way over, they could talk to each other for a change, without interruption from the telephone. Now that Dot has managed to hook up Viola and Mrs. Tran—at least, she hopes she has—she's all about killing two birds with one stone.

38

The Tran Family at the Door

Dot shows up at Viola's before their first meeting with Mrs. Tran, as promised, and when she answers the door, standing there are not only Mrs. Tran but also Jim and Mr. Tran, trailed by Viola's neighbor, in her curlers. "I heard a commotion out in the hallway," the neighbor calls past the Trans to Viola. "And whaddya know, there's a pack of Middle Easterners, or whatever they are, rapping on your door. I thought I'd better make sure you're okay."

"These are my guests. Not a *pack*," says Viola, dismissing her. "But thank you for your concern."

"If that's how you feel. But don't say I didn't warn you."

"Wow," says Mrs. Tran after she leaves. She walks over to Viola, who is ensconced in her armchair. "Put up your arm, please. The good one."

Puzzled, Viola raises her arm, and Mrs. Tran slaps her a high five. Viola looks astonished, and Jim and Mr. Tran burst out laughing. "She learned that from me!" says Jim.

"We do it in our family," says Mr. Tran, and he and Jim slap each other's hands as a further demonstration.

"It means, *good job*," Mrs. Tran explains.

"Middle Easterners," Viola repeats. "What an idiot. Please, let's start over." She holds out her hand, and Mrs. Tran shakes it. "Viola Cottage. Nice to meet you."

"Mai Tran," Mrs. Tran introduces herself. "My husband, Bao. My son, Jim." She raises her eyebrows and looks at Dot. "And you? What is your interest?"

"I work with Jim at the library—Dot Greenbaum? I spoke to Mr. Tran on the phone?"

"Of course. Jim has told us all about you," says Mr. Tran.

"Uh-oh," says Dot.

"No, no, we are glad to meet you," he says. "Jim loves the library. The children. Even his boss." He smiles.

In fact, Mr. and Mrs. Tran don't look so different from the way Dot first imagined them, with their round glasses and identical heights. Of course, she towers over them. She is a giant ugly American. Mr. Tran's crewcut is gray, but Mrs. Tran's bob is still dark, with only a few silver threads, which Dot is relieved to notice. After Jim's account of his mother's anxieties, Dot had worried that she would be frail and frightened, and that Dot would feel guilty to see her scurrying around the apartment at Viola's command. But Dot can see already that Mrs. Tran is not someone to *scurry*. What a word.

"Tea, anyone?" announces Viola.

"I will get it," says Mrs. Tran. "I want to check your kitchen."

"Check! I don't see why . . ." Viola starts to protest. But she stops herself. It's nice to be waited on, the way her imaginary companion would have done. "Okay, thank you, Mrs. Tran."

Until now, they have all been standing around Viola's chair, but when Viola agrees to let Mrs. Tran bring her tea, Dot feels so relieved that she collapses into the seat next to her. Between Viola's resistance and Mrs. Tran's concerns about American immigration authorities, and Americans in general, Dot was not certain that the arrangement, as logical and convenient as it should have been, would ever come to pass. The neighbor's interference had the positive result of aligning Viola with the Trans, and Mrs. Tran's forthright and determined manner seems to have impressed Viola. Jim and Mr. Tran also take seats. *They must feel relieved too*, thinks Dot.

"No paperwork," Mr. Tran reminds Viola.

"Of course not," she agrees. "It's completely unnecessary."

"And pay in cash."

"I suppose I can manage that."

"Mr. Tran will drop me off on weekday mornings, on his way to work, and pick me up in the afternoon. I do not drive anymore," says Mrs. Tran. "If you need that, you must find someone else."

"No, no," says Viola. "That arrangement will be fine. I have my food and such delivered."

Mrs. Tran walks into the kitchen and calls back to Viola, "As I can see. You have many containers in here. When I start working for you, first thing, I will do some cleaning. It is unsanitary for such an old person to live this way."

"I'm sorry," says Viola—to Dot's surprise. Viola is not given to apologies or explanations. Or to letting someone else take charge. But there's Viola, face reddening, as a stranger passes judgment, noting the mess and, probably, the spots on her sweater. Viola is embarrassed, Dot realizes. She's lost control. It's probably the reason she didn't want anyone in her home in the first place. That, and the disruption of her private routines, whatever they are. Viola often tells Dot how busy she is, but she doesn't say with what.

"Don't worry," Mrs. Tran tells Viola kindly. "You would be surprised at the things I see. People don't think they need the help of a trained nurse like me."

Dot believes that in Viola's situation, she would never let things get to this point—but really, no one can predict such a thing.

39

An Item

Susan and Cynthia are an item. Or at least, that's how Susan sees it, and she is pretty sure Cynthia would agree, although they haven't yet had the serious conversation about their status that is apparently required of all lesbians. Or of all people? She wouldn't know. To her, that sort of agonizing mutual analysis has always seemed like a particularly lesbian-ish way of going about a relationship—and not her favorite, if only she had a choice. Right now, the Cynthia thing is fun, and Susan would like to keep it that way. It's too soon for the tears and giggles and suddenly monogamous and meaningful sex of the commitment discussion—although not too soon to be able to count on a Saturday night date that lasts pleasantly into Sunday afternoon or even over Sunday night, with a dramatic rush early Monday morning to usher Cynthia out of Susan's unit unnoticed.

Because Cynthia doesn't want anyone at Maple Grove copping to the relationship just yet. She has an uncomfortable feeling that it may violate a rule—sexually exploiting a resident or some such thing. Not that she's exploiting! Susan could hardly be more willing. But Mrs. Dailey might not view it that way. She was never fond of lesbians, and she's worse lately, since her adventure with Mr. Belrose.

Neither Susan nor Cynthia minds the secrecy, for now. It adds a shiver of excitement to their trysts, and for Susan, it means that she can wait for an opportune moment to reveal to Dot and Ralfie what she's been getting up to at the so-called Grave. Ta-da!

Meanwhile, Maggy and Shirl have been attempting to interrogate Cynthia ever since their night at the Rooster. She should have known what the agenda was when Maggy invited her, and her alone, out for a postwork drink.

"So, how far along are you?" Maggy asks.

"That's what people say when you're pregnant!"

"You know what I mean, Cyn. The New Chick. What stage is it at? Can't keep your hands to yourselves? Regular sleepovers? Confessions of love? Exchanging rings?"

"Of course we're not exchanging rings! I've known her for what? A month and a half?"

"Nothing wrong with it." Maggy waves her left hand at Cynthia, to show off her amethyst solitaire. "Me and Shirl, we've had these since forever. Purple's our color."

"I thought your color was plaid," says Cynthia. She has always thought the flashy ring looks incongruous on Maggy's chubby, nail-bitten finger, especially together with her usual outfit of flannel or fleece.

"Ho ho," says Maggy. "Good one. You got me there."

"What can I say, Mags? I like her. A lot, actually."

"But that's awesome! You deserve it, you know?"

"People deserve a lot of things," says Cynthia darkly. "They don't always get them."

"Oh, please, don't go all philosophical on me. Come to dinner. This weekend, okay? Shirl wants to see you. Bring the chick."

"Susan, you mean."

"Yeah, Susan. Bring her. I'm barbecuing."

So now Cynthia is at the wheel, and Susan cannot tell, as they drive and drive, when they leave one suburb and cross into the next, since the pattern of alternating housing developments and malls seems to stretch on endlessly, unbounded. Maggy and Shirl, it turns out, live in a townhome. Contemplating the tall, narrow structure renews Susan's appreciation for her unit. At least it's all on one floor. If Dot had to climb up and down all those stairs, she would definitely never visit—although, Susan reminds herself, Dot never visits anyway. Susan is the one who ends up traveling back and forth on the cursed Route 95, with its inexplicable traffic and surreal signage. She follows Cynthia around the building to a patio in the back, where Maggy, as promised, is standing proudly at an enormous gas grill, spatula at the ready, monitoring an array of sizzling burgers—far more, it seems to Susan, than needed to feed the four of them.

"How do you like this baby?" Maggy gestures at the grill. "It's her first time out for a spin."

"I'll miss the flaming lighter fluid," says Cynthia.

"Pyro!" calls Shirl from a lawn chair positioned away from the smoke. She waves Susan and Cynthia over to a couple of additional chairs. "Welcome! Take a load off. One of these days, I swear our old grill was going to burn down the house. Or our old *girl!*" She turns to Maggy. "Get it, Mags? Old grill? Old girl?"

"No," says Maggy.

"Ha," says Shirl. "Of course she gets it. So, I picked this one up on sale. Not as exciting, I give you that." Shirl reaches into a cooler by her side and tosses Cynthia a can of beer. Apparently used to this trick, Cynthia catches it one-handed. Susan leans in close to Shirl's chair and holds out a hand, and Shirl tosses one to her, too. "Great to see you again, Susie. We had some good times, didn't we?"

"Sure," says Susan, confused by the plural, since they've met only once. And no one has ever called her Susie before. It makes her wonder about how Shirl sees her. Her personality doesn't usually lend itself to diminutives.

Maggy interrupts them. "Stand back! I'm flipping 'em!" she yells, as though she's mastered the trick of making the burgers fly through the air and land on a plate—and maybe she had, at the charcoal grill. At this new one, though, she wiggles the spatula under each burger and turns it over carefully.

"Looking good, Mags," says Shirl. "They've got grill marks and everything. I hope you guys are hungry."

"I just want to wash up first," says Susan.

"Door off the kitchen," Shirl directs her. "Next to the stairs."

And that's when Susan sees it.

A chairlift, winding around gracefully to follow the shape of each flight. The lift is constructed from modules, some straight, some curved, that fit together like Legos. Why did they all assume Ralfie knew what she was talking about?

Susan can't wait to tell Dot. Not to mention Ralfie.

Back outside, she learns the whole story: how Shirl broke her ankle falling on the ice during that awful winter a couple of years ago, a bad break—although what sort of break would be good?—requiring two surgeries, which put her in a boot and off her feet for so long that her whole leg shriveled up. Creepy, and she had to do months of strengthening therapy to learn to walk again. Maggy bought her a very cool wooden cane with a beautiful carved head, but it wasn't the right height, so her back went out, and she had to switch to an ugly adjustable metal cane from the hospital. The old-lady kind, with feet.

She still uses it sometimes, when her ankle acts up in bad weather.

"Which is all the time, around here," says Maggy. "And she was so unsteady, I had the lift put in. Better safe, you know."

"But I don't usually need it," Shirl protests. "Not anymore."

"I just never got around to taking it out," says Maggy. "And it's kind of a blast, when you've been running around all day and you don't want to take another step, or you're carrying laundry up from the basement. You sit down and make yourself nice and comfie, and it cranks you right up."

"I thought you could only use those things on a straight flight of stairs," says Susan.

"Nah," says Maggy. "They make them to fit, whatever. You can get anything if you pay for it."

40

Ralfie Does Not Insist

Ralfie is so pleased with the news about the chairlift that she doesn't even attempt to insist, in defiance of the facts, that she was right all along. It is not only a gadget; it's a supergadget, which probably breaks down, requiring investigations into its workings and special tools for tinkering with it. And of course, by the way, there's its usefulness. Her knees. "I guess we don't need to buy into Viola's building after all. I'll let the guy at the bank know I don't need to withdraw our money," she tells Dot.

"What guy at the bank?" says Dot, horrified. Dot wants to shake her, an impulse that is even more horrifying than Ralfie's comment. Dot has never thought of herself as the kind of person who would lay violent hands on anyone—on Ralfie, of all people. "Rafaella! What did you do?

"Nothing! He said I should mull it over, talk to you—"

"I don't remember talking—"

"Keep your shirt on. Jeez. I was going to, I just didn't get a chance—"

"I cannot believe this!" Dot tries to remember—has Ralfie ever gone behind her back like this? Liquidating their IRAs, on her own, telling Dot nothing—it's like stealing! Except she never got around to it. "We decided Viola's building was impossible! How could you!"

"*You* decided. But forget it, that's over," says Ralfie airily, waving away Dot's concern. "We just install one of those curve-around-type lifts, like Susan says, and stay here, like you always wanted."

"*We*," Dot corrects her. "Like *we* always wanted."

"Okay, *we*. It probably wouldn't have worked out so great living next door to your old flame anyway."

"Old *flame*?" says Dot disingenuously, trying not to panic. There's Ralfie. In her corner. Viola, in hers. Compartmentalization! It's easy. Practical, even. At some point, Dot had stopped giving much thought to the flare-up that happens when two bare wires touch and short out.

"Well, yeah, Dotty. All these years. I'm not an idiot."

"No," says Dot, slowly. "You are not an idiot."

"You never brought it up, so I figured I'd keep my mouth shut."

"Didn't you mind?" says Dot, full-on guilty.

"Yeah, I minded! Some. At first." Dot would conscientiously inform her whenever she had a lunch date with Viola, just the two of them, old pals, and Ralfie would claim it was a-okay with her not to be invited; she had less than zero interest in Dot's librarian friends, with their gossip about other librarians and their chatter about books they had read, movies they had seen.

Even when Ralfie had seen the same movies, and read some of the books, too, she could never seem to find a footing in their conversations. Her personal taste ran to biographies and battles, anyway, not novels— that is, when she was not studying up on her job skills. Basic engineering, personnel management, carpentry and plumbing: the DPW was no piece of cake, whatever the librarians might have thought of it. "But we were good together, and I figured, 'Why rock the boat?'"

There was a time when Dot had suspected Ralfie of having an affair, although Ralfie insisted it was overtime, and it's true it was during the middle of a bad winter, successive nor'easters, one on the heels of another, and many of those late nights Ralfie looked honestly exhausted when she finally walked in the door, sweaty yet also shivering, her Patriots hat askew. Ralfie's in the clear, Dot thinks, which is more than she can say for herself. For a moment, she considers trying to deny the whole thing. Discards that idea. There's nothing she can say for herself. "I'm such a hypocrite. How can you stand me?"

"You dope, Dotty," says Ralfie. "You still don't get it. You're my one and only! I'll never understand the attraction of that old bat, but as long as I'm the one you come home to . . . Anyway, I figured it would cool down after a while."

After a decade or two, thinks Dot. But it's a relief, kind of, to have it all out in the open. To unburden herself of her secrets. "You were right," she says. "Viola and I, we're not having—"

Ralfie sticks her fingers in her ears, shakes her head back and forth, and starts chanting, "LALALALALA! I can't hear you!"

"Ralfie! What—"

"No details, okay? I have my limits."

"I'm sorry," says Dot, relieved to have done something she can clearly and immediately apologize for. "I'll never—"

"And don't make me any promises. Who knows if you can keep them. Just love me."

"I do love you!" How is it, she marvels, that she has not ruined her life? A great job, a great place to live, a great relationship, she remembers. Three out of three. She sighs. "You'll never trust me again, will you."

"Oh, maybe, maybe not." Ralfie laughs. "You've got that roving eye."

As though she's proud of Dot for it, thinks Dot. There's Ralfie for you, finding something to crow about in a person's worst behavior. But who would've thought Dot would turn out to be the one, in their relationship? The hot ticket. The explorer of new territories. Dot almost feels proud of herself too.

41

Expedition #2

Susan and Ralfie have become allies for once, both clamoring for an expedition to Maggy and Shirl's, to see the curve-around lift in action. "And," Susan adds, "you could meet Cynthia."

"We already did," says Dot. "On our tour."

"Re-meet her, then. That time doesn't count. You probably don't even remember what she looks like."

Susan is right. Dot wouldn't recognize Cynthia if she waltzed in on Susan's arm—which would surely be a clue. All she remembers is an enormous flower arrangement.

Dot doesn't want to meet the girlfriend and check out the chairlift. Since she and Ralfie aired their secrets, they are good, maybe even better than before—but Dot can't help feeling that it's all a little wobbly. And Susan's relationship, her friends, even the lift, just mean more changes—new people, new interactions, even a new way of maneuvering around her home. These are *good* changes, Dot reminds herself. Ralfie does not need her cane only occasionally, like Susan's apparently new best friend, Shirl; she needs it all the time. With the lift, she could stop struggling. Dot could breathe.

And if change, of any sort, is Dot's problem, then she is not on her way to getting old; she has arrived, she reprimands herself. Like the geriatrics in the chairlift ad on TV. She imagines herself and Ralfie in their places: Ralfie rising up the stairs wearing the old guy's cardigan, Dot watching from the landing in a flowered dress and orthopedic shoes the color of bandaids. For some reason, in this vision she and Ralfie are both wearing curly gray wigs, nothing like their hair in real life, perched askew on their heads. Dot shakes her head to rid herself of the absurd image.

Get used to it, she thinks. She wanted to Age in Place? It's not a fantasy anymore; it's for real, with canes and chairlifts. Senior fares. Grabbing the handicapped seats on the bus. Exercising but in moderation. Swallowing pricey ginkgo biloba and fish oil capsules, although these have been scientifically proven to do exactly nothing to enhance memory. But you never know.

So, another expedition. Any reason Dot can think of not to go is, she recognizes, completely spurious. When she and Ralfie arrive at Maple Grove, Susan is sitting on the front desk, in intimate conversation with Cynthia, who is at her post behind it. "I screwed up," says Susan, sliding off the desk. Dot had assumed Cynthia was coming with them—Maggy and Shirl are her friends, after all—but now it turns out that Cynthia has to work. Awkward.

"Not your fault, baby. Mrs. Daily changed my schedule again." Cynthia turns to Dot and Ralfie. "You know what she's like, you met her. Her spidey sense tingles whenever I have plans—"

"Anyway, here is my big sis!" says Susan, putting an arm around Dot and giving her an unexpected squeeze.

Cynthia leans across the desk to shake Dot's hand. "Hey, I've heard all about you, Big Sis. Sometimes I envy Susan, having such a great family."

"And this is Ralfie," Susan adds. Ralfie sticks out her hand.

"Sure, hi!" Cynthia shakes it and continues, intent on making her point. "I have my chosen family, you know, Maggy and Shirl, but you guys had it right from the start."

"I guess we don't always realize how lucky we are," says Dot.

"No, we don't," says Susan. "At least, not some of us."

"My buddy Mags is dying to show you the lift," says Cynthia. "It was a godsend for Shirl, you'll love it, and them too—you'll see."

"Hope so," says Dot.

When they pull up, Maggy and Shirl burst out the front door, as though they've been lying in wait behind it. House-proud, they lead their visitors through the living room and kitchen and finally to the main event.

Before they can say anything, Susan points it out with a sweep of her arm. "This is it! Aren't you glad I discovered it?"

"You and Columbus," mutters Ralfie. "Going around discovering. At least he was a *paisan*."

"What?" says Susan.

"Come on, take a spin," Maggy offers Ralfie, so she, then Dot, and then for good measure Susan and Maggy and Shirl all take turns riding up and down.

"As you can see, she works great," says Maggy. "Even around the loop-de-loops. You just have to keep her maintained. Oiled and such."

Ralfie nods appreciatively, and Maggy and Shirl lead them outside to view the grill, which Ralfie also admires.

"Maggy here put it together, you know," says Shirl. "It came in about a million pieces, with just a diagram, and instructions in Japanese. But that's Mags. Handy as anything."

"Have to be," says Maggy. "It's not like we can call our husband."

"This suburban living might not be so bad," says Ralfie, exasperating Susan.

"Like I've tried to tell you!"

"But who would've thought there'd be all these lesbians up here, and a bar and everything?"

"Not me," says Dot. She is absolutely not going to let Susan try again to convince them that they should move up here, no matter how pleasant the suburbs might seem on a sunny afternoon on the patio, with Susan's new friends offering around cold drinks and sandwiches. The damn chairlift, she thinks. Okay, it will help. At least until something else goes wrong, and the exact nature of that, and what they might need to do about it, is so unpredictable it's not even worth worrying about—except she can't stop herself. "Thanks, you guys," she tells Maggy and Shirl. "You've given us a lot to think about."

Back in the car with Ralfie at the wheel, Dot, riding shotgun, can feel Susan glaring at her from the back seat, although Dot can't understand why, since as far as she can see, the afternoon went great. The chairlift proved to be everything Susan said it would be, and Dot and Ralfie enthusiastically expressed their appreciation. Everybody got along. Dot turns around. "Good people," she tells Susan.

"Especially that Mags," Ralfie agrees. "She showed me how she arranges her workbench, with all her tools, you can tell she actually uses them."

"She's a contractor," says Susan. "Of course she has tools."

"No kidding," says Ralfie. "I had no idea. I bet she can recommend someone who installs those things, down our way."

"Probably," says Susan. As pleased as she was to show Dot and Ralfie the chairlift, she is annoyed that they haven't said anything to her about Cynthia—another of her discoveries in the supposed wasteland of Maple Grove. "So, what do you think of my new girlfriend?" she breaks down and asks.

"Nice," says Dot. "Of course, we didn't get much of a chance to talk."

"You could've tried!" Susan bursts out. "You guys were supposedly so sorry for me, stuck by myself at Maple Grove—and here I show you that's not even true, about being stuck, and I figure out what to do about your dinky third-floor apartment, and you don't even care! She was looking forward to meeting you."

"I'm sorry! I didn't realize—" says Dot.

"You were quick enough to drive up to Maggy and Shirl's when you thought they had something for you, but you never visit me, or even listen when I tell you what's happening in my life; you just have your own ideas about what it's like." Susan stops talking and stares out the window. "Oh, forget it."

"Hey, like I said, I liked them," says Ralfie. "I'd go up there to visit them again, and you too, why not—"

"But Susan . . ." Dot sighs, then decides she will not point out that it was Susan who scheduled their expedition for a date when Cynthia had to work; nor will she protest that her apartment is not *dinky*. Maple Grove is working out for Susan. Good for her! But sometimes it seems to Dot that Susan will feel truly happy only when she has nudged everyone into line and has them following her lead. She has the herding instincts of a border collie.

"I told you, forget it, okay?" Susan repeats.

"Okay then." Dot shrugs, and they drive the rest of the way in silence.

They pull up to Maple Grove's grand portico, and Susan gets out of the car. "Bye," she concedes.

"Yeah, bye," says Dot.

"Bye," says Ralfie.

Susan slams the car door, harder, it seems to Dot, than necessary. Dot knows she should insist on dialogue, and offer to—something. Take Cynthia out for a drink? Buy her a present? Send her an arrangement of congratulatory flowers? Dot is a lesbian, for god's sake. She has no practice at being a sister-in-law. Although Susan does, after all these years of Ralfie, so she would be the perfect person for Dot to ask for advice, but . . .

42

Recuperating

Back home, Dot and Ralfie climb up to their apartment and are recuperating on the couch in the living room. "I've had it with this," pants Ralfie. "I'm calling that Maggy in the morning and getting some names. Good thing your sister mentioned she's a contractor. It's perfect. Meanwhile, you'll sweet-talk the neighbors—"

"Won't the construction interfere with the Complaint Department?" Dot interrupts. She hadn't figured on jumping into this so quickly, somehow having lost sight of the fact that once Ralfie decides on something, she's all in.

"Jeez, Dot, I can walk and chew gum at the same time."

Dot tries to focus on the positive, but problems keep flooding her mind. Like, the neighbors. The neighbors don't need a chairlift, and the stairs are common property. They would all have to agree to it. In all this time, she and Ralfie have never had a conflict with the neighbors. They have a condo meeting once a year or so, with rotating hosts, and it is all very amicable, tea and cake—but installing a lift is not like fixing the roof, which you have no choice about, if you don't want the building to fall down around your ears. She and Ralfie could promise to pay for it, Dot supposes. No one else would have to chip in a dime.

But that's another thing. If the lift has to go around turns, it has to be custom-built. It will probably cost more than they have ever paid for anything, except the apartment itself. But that's the point, Dot reminds herself. We'll be able to stay in our apartment. And however much it costs, it can't possibly be as expensive as a condo in Viola's building. She knows she should be happy. Relieved. But the way ahead is bumpy, not as clear as Ralfie seems to think. "I need a nap," she tells Ralfie. "All that driving," she lies.

"Why the long face?" Ralfie calls after her. Dot ignores her and disappears into the bedroom. "A horse walks into a bar," calls Ralfie, although she knows Dot can't hear her. Shouldn't Dot, like Ralfie, be ready to celebrate, now that the problem of the stairs is no longer *insurmountable*? Ha! And yet, there's Dot, moping around. Ralfie could tell she was unhappy, back at Maggy and Shirl's, which was really too bad, since Ralfie was digging it. The girls were old school, like you don't often meet these days. A butch who can put together a grill with not a screw left over, and her admiring girlfriend. And then, all of a sudden, the afternoon was done, and they got up and left.

Lying in the darkened bedroom, Dot thinks: *Down-hearted. Heart-sick.* So many heart-words for feeling blue. She thought she had conquered it, walking, going back to work. But here it is again, enveloping her, even though objectively, things are looking up. She and Ralfie have jobs, a minuscule mortgage, a bank account. They will buy a chairlift. Viola has hired Mrs. Tran. Jim is back at the library. Ralfie is off the truck. So, why the long face? A question even the resourceful Dot can't answer.

43

A Big Honking Piece of Machinery

But Dot is right, at least about one thing. The neighbors do not want a big honking piece of machinery blocking their stairs. And what if there's a fire? They have many meetings, at first with the tea and cake, and later without the friendly snacks, and finally Dot comes up with a compromise. The lift will go up only one flight, from the second floor to the third. No one on the lower floors ever ventures up that high except maybe to borrow a lemon. And if they need one that badly, they can enjoy the ride. Dot and Ralfie figure that this arrangement will be better than nothing, since it's that last flight that really gets you. Building a lift just for one floor will cut down on the expense, at least a little, although the thing will still have to negotiate a tricky curve up to the third-floor landing.

If there's a fire, Ralfie says, there's always the back stairs. In a panic they can manage them. She remembers flying down the stairs when Dot had her heart attack. Adrenaline.

So Dot can barely remember when, leaving for the library, she was not greeted by a couple of workers in big dusty boots sitting on the stairs drinking coffee and chatting with Ralfie. She has been spending her days standing in the apartment doorway with her cell phone in a holster, alternately interrogating the guys about what they are doing, and taking calls about potholes, graffiti, and why the new streetlight has been erected in the exact place to block the corner stop sign from the view of oncoming traffic.

"I had no idea it would take this long," Dot tells the guys early one morning, on her way to visit Viola. She wants to check on her and Mrs. Tran and see how the arrangement is working out.

"We're trying to finish up and get out of here," the supervisor tells her. "But we gotta get it right, we don't want it falling apart with you nice ladies sitting in it."

"No, of course not. We'd sue the pants off you."

"Ha ha." He laughs uncomfortably.

Arriving at Viola's, Dot can feel the tension in the room as soon as Mrs. Tran opens the door. Viola calls out from her chair, "I could have done that myself, Mai. I am still capable of walking across the room."

"No, no," says Mrs. Tran. "You are a fall risk. Your doc says. You fainted and—"

"I beg to differ! I am not a risk. I am an adult human being, capable of answering my own door!"

"Not what your doctor said!" says Mrs. Tran. She turns to Dot. "You see how she is."

"And don't talk about me behind my back!" says Viola. "To my best friend, of all people!" To Dot she complains, "I had no idea she would be so—so sneaky!"

"Um," says Dot, thinking of her own failings. "Isn't that a sort of stereotype?"

"Do not accuse me, Dotty! I'm trying to tell you about my experience with this person so highly recommended by you."

"But she said it right in front of you, not behind your back. And she's just trying to reinforce what your doctor told you. That's her job."

"Exactly," says Mrs. Tran. "I am doing my best."

"Of course you are, dear," says Viola.

Dot stares at Viola, confused by her change in attitude.

"I'm just difficult," says Viola complacently. "Mai, would you kindly get us some coffee?"

"Sure," says Mrs. Tran.

When she goes into the kitchen, Dot says to Viola, "What is going on here?"

"Don't be such a worrywart. Mai and I are like an old married couple."

"But you're not married! She works for you. All that yelling was really disturbing."

"It's just the way we talk to each other. You've seen how people yell in Chinatown."

"Mrs. Tran is not Chinese," Dot can't help pointing out, although she immediately realizes that this is the wrong answer.

"Many Vietnamese have Chinese roots," says Viola smugly.

Mrs. Tran comes back into the room and hands around mugs of coffee to Viola and Dot. "Black okay?" she asks Dot. "We have no cream."

"Thanks, black is perfect," says Dot. It isn't really—she takes hers light and sweet—but she wants to give Mrs. Tran a compliment.

Mrs. Tran shakes her head. "Vietnamese coffee is made with condensed milk. It is delicious. Not like this, which is so bitter."

"That is much too fattening, Mai," says Viola. "We don't drink it that way in this country."

"Mrs. Tran," says Dot. "I want to thank you. Viola seems so much better since you've been coming. And the apartment is so orderly."

"Yes," says Viola. "In fact, I hardly need help at all anymore. The cast comes off my arm next week."

"So this posting is ending soon?" says Mrs. Tran. She sounds hopeful.

"All good things, you know," says Viola.

Mrs. Tran collects the mugs. "Let me help," says Dot, following her into the kitchen. "Do you really think Viola is safe to be on her own?" she asks. "It's not just about the arm. What about her mind? She never used to be so bossy and insensitive." She thinks of Viola's stained sweater.

"Maybe she did not show you this side," says Mrs. Tran. "To me she seems same as always."

"I think she still needs you. I'll try to figure something out. Don't cross her off your schedule just yet."

"She is not an easy client," says Mrs. Tran. "But I can deal. Although the money—"

"Thank you," says Dot. She will give Mrs. Tran a little bonus, she decides, and pretend it came from Viola. Something to persuade Mrs. Tran to stay on. And then she'll tell Viola the doctor insists. It's very inconvenient, thinks Dot, to have to lie to people for their own good.

44

When They Were Kids

When Dot and Susan were kids, the people next door used to set up a pool when the weather got hot. Everybody was invited. When the kids got bored with paddling around in circles, they would stand, take in a big breath, hold their noses, and squat. They would pop up one by one, sputtering, and there would be Susan, sitting calmly on the plastic floor, her hair waving around her in the turquoise water. Dot didn't like this game. Susan would rather drown herself than lose.

"What do you think we should do?" Dot asks Ralfie one evening when she arrives home from work. Susan's been keeping radio silence, and when Dot calls, she doesn't pick up. This afternoon, the library was quiet—it was Jim's turn to handle story hour—which gave Dot the time to feel worse and worse about their estrangement. She doesn't really think Ralfie will have any constructive advice, and in fact Dot usually knows better than to consult her about Susan-problems, but she has to spill the worries churning around in her head to somebody.

"Let her cool her heels for a while," says Ralfie. "It won't hurt her."

"But it's hurting me!"

"Aw, baby," says Ralfie. It's late afternoon—twilight, when the shadows make it difficult to distinguish one object from another. The sky is a hazy violet-gray, and for a change Ralfie is not chatting up the guys in the stairwell or filling in complaint forms on her computer. She's resting on the couch with her bad leg propped up on a pillow. "Come here." She scoots over and pats the cushion next to her. "This stress ain't no good for you." Dot sits, and Ralfie strokes her hair. "Don't let her get to you," she murmurs into Dot's ear, and kisses her neck. "That's just what she wants."

Dot stretches her neck, to facilitate more kissing. She didn't expect the conversation to take this turn, but she's going with it. "And you?" she flirts. "What do you want?"

"You know."

"Tell me."

"How about I show you?" Ralfie takes Dot's shoulders, gently pushes her down on the couch, and starts to crawl on top of her. But her weight is on the wrong knee. She yelps. Takes a breath. Shifts. "Sorry."

"Ow! Your elbow! Now you're jabbing my tit." Dot sits up, leans around Ralfie to get Ralfie's cane. "Here. I think we'll do better in the bedroom."

"For a minute there, I thought you were going to punish me!" says Ralfie hopefully.

"Oh, come on. When have we ever been into that?"

"I remember one time—" Ralfie waggles her eyebrows.

"A hundred years ago, in the nineties! Everybody was trying it! Anyway, I was drunk; it was after whatshername's annual Samhain party—"

"I'd never seen you like that—"

"Somebody doctored the punch, I've never had such a headache. Anyway, we were playing with scarves, not canes."

"Ha! Your knots came undone—"

"They did not!"

"They did! I pretended I was still tied up so you could—"

"That's what you say now—"

"It's just too bad you were never a boy scout."

"I am not going to try beating you with your own cane!"

"You're probably right." Ralfie sighs. "I'm beat up enough already."

In bed there's more room, so no more awkward poking. And Ralfie has always been brilliant at foreplay; she knows how to touch Dot, and exactly when the moment has come to tweak her nipple and make her body light up like a Christmas tree.

"Love, you make me happy," Dot says with a sigh.

"Even after all this time?"

"Mm-hmm," says Dot, giving Ralfie a lazy kiss on the cheek and turning her around to spoon her. "Even after all this time."

"You're so vanilla," says Ralfie.

"Just like you," says Dot, reaching down to rest her hand on a certain place on Ralfie's ass. She feels her relax.

And maybe Dot and Ralfie's good sex vibes have an effect, because afterward, when they've lazed in bed for a while and then ordered in a pizza, since they are suddenly ravenous, Dot's phone rings, and it's Susan. Of all people. "I just got your messages. My phone was busted, I've been spending half my life in the Apple store."

Dot doesn't believe this for a minute.

"All the kids there are so adorable. Is that a legal hiring practice, do you think? At least they're very diverse . . ."

Ralfie hands Dot a slice on a paper plate, and Dot bites off the point. "What about Cynthia?" she says, muffled by pizza, as she catches a lengthening string of mozzarella between thumb and forefinger.

"What do you mean, 'What about Cynthia?' The Apple store has nothing to do with Cynthia, I was just making an observation. And I hope my phone's not going bad again. I can barely understand you."

"It's pizza night," explains Dot. She points at the beer Ralfie is drinking, and Ralfie pops one open, slurps the foam from the top of the can, and hands it to her.

"What's all that weird noise?" says Susan.

"Nothing," says Dot. "So tell me, what's up?"

"You tell me! Why did you leave all those messages?"

"Last time we saw each other, we didn't end on such great terms, remember?"

Susan sighs. "Oh, Dotty. My life's a wreck. Germaine, Cynthia—"

"Cynthia?"

"She says she's not into commitment. But I wasn't asking for that!"

"But you must've said—"

"Vacation! I said, 'Let's plan our vacation.'"

"Maybe she doesn't like Provincetown?"

"She *loves* Provincetown. That's how the vacation idea came up in the first place. We were comparing notes—East End, West End. The old Pied bar, remember, Dotty? When it was women only?"

Dot laughs. "Me and Ralfie had no money for a room. We would camp and bring a big cooler with ice, make a couple of G&Ts before we went out, so we didn't have to spend much on drinks. No wonder the bar went coed."

"I told Cynthia, 'Let's go.' And she starts hesitating, and finally she says, 'Summer's months from now.'"

"Uh-oh," says Dot. Maybe, she thinks, Susan's phone really was broken. Even if she was still mad at Dot, she would have wanted to talk about something like this.

"Uh-huh," says Susan. "She goes, 'Who knows what'll happen between now and then.' And I tell her, 'The good places are all taken if you don't get in early. Everybody knows that.' So she says, 'I just don't want to be *tied down*.' Quote-unquote! It's very uncomfortable, Dotty! When she's at the front desk, she won't even say hi. Just looks through me like I'm not there."

Bad planning, thinks Dot. Getting involved with someone you can't avoid if things go south. Not that she can blame her. Nobody anticipates this sort of problem, not at the exciting beginning.

"I think she was looking for an excuse. We were happy, I think it scared her."

Dot nods. "Some people can't trust that they've got a good thing. So they wreck it. But you know what? She'll come around. I predict it."

"I don't know—"

Dot nods; she's convinced herself. "I'm absolutely sure of it. You'll see."

"I guess it's on me. I'll get in her face. Make her talk to me—"

"Exactly," says Dot. "Tell her how you feel about her."

"Love," says Susan. "I don't know if we're there yet. But I'll try." She hesitates. "Thanks, sis. You're a pal."

After Dot hangs up, Ralfie says, "Lucky we got over to Maggy and Shirl's that day, before the big breakup."

"Is that all you can think of, you heartless thing?" says Dot, fake-punching Ralfie on the shoulder.

"Just saying," says Ralfie.

They tussle pleasantly for a bit, and then Dot stops and says, "Poor Susan. I feel for her. Really. She'll power through eventually, but she's torn up about it, I can tell."

45

Finished

The chairlift is finished. The guys have packed away their tools and vacuumed up the dust, mostly, and they knock on the door to say good-bye. Dot's already left for work, so it's just Ralfie, shaking hands all around, and telling them, "Don't be a stranger"—although she knows she'll never see them again.

Without them, the building is very quiet. Ralfie looks at the lift. It's big—bigger than it seemed when the guys were putting it together. It blocks the stairs, just as the neighbors predicted, but you can squeeze around it if you have to. Cautiously, Ralfie sits down and pushes the start button. The mechanism hums to life, and her chair begins to move across the landing. Startled, she grips the arm rests, and the chair descends, slowly, elegantly, a step at a time. *I could get down faster on my own two feet*, she thinks, but stops herself, remembers: her two feet don't carry her so well anymore. She needs Dot's arm to lean on, or her cane, or best case, both.

So there's Ralfie. Somehow she never believed it would come to this, although of course it does, for everyone. *Nothing special about old Ralfie*, she thinks. Join the rest of the human race. But slowly, hobbling ever forward.

46

The Ducky

Dot puts on a light jacket and sneakers to go for a walk. On weekend days like this—warm, sunny, with a light cooling breeze—she tries to make it twice around the pond. Lately, she has to share the path with extremely large, aggressive birds, strutting around like they own the place: Canada geese, wild turkeys. There used to be a great blue heron who fished quietly from his own little beach, but he was mauled by an unleashed German shepherd, causing an uproar in the neighborhood, some taking the part of the bird, some of the dog. This afternoon, Dot passes what seems to be an inordinate number of people with children: a white lesbian couple with an apparently adopted Chinese child toddling between them, holding their hands; a pair of grandmothers gossiping in Spanish with each other and reprimanding in English the two pink-tutued girls darting ahead of them; a Black man with long dreads proudly displaying the infant bound to his chest; a gray-haired lady pulling not a child but an extremely obedient poodle in a wagon. It's all very cheerful, and Dot feels buoyed by the idea that she will live in this lovely community for the foreseeable future.

She remembers her walks to school as a child, when even the sidewalk slabs had certain meanings, not necessarily benign. That game: *step on a crack/break your mother's back*. She used to find things: pennies, a red leaf, a stone that glittered like gold. She pocketed them but often lost them even before she arrived home. Slowing her pace, Dot tries to re-create the wandering mood of childhood.

There's a whirr of tires, and turning to look behind her, she sees a young woman—in fantastic shape, even after child-bearing, wearing tights and a fitted windbreaker—pushing a three-wheeled jogging stroller. As she runs past, her baby flings something out of the stroller, hitting Dot in the chest. She bends to pick it up—it's a thoroughly chewed rubber ducky, not quite as yellow as it was originally. The woman with the stroller is by now too far ahead of Dot to hear her call out, so she sticks the ducky in her jacket pocket, continues her walk, and forgets about it.

Dot rarely wears that particular jacket—it's not really suited for the unpredictable New England chill—and months later, when she does, and puts her hand in the pocket, instead of a crumpled and possibly used tissue, she finds the ducky. A thing life threw at her.

As Viola once pointed out to Dot, neither of them can look forward to being cared for by their children, nor is there a younger generation coming up to inherit. Years after this walk of Dot's, when hauling themselves up even two flights of stairs has become more than she and Ralfie can manage, they move into Viola's old apartment, left to Dot in Viola's will, along with her scarf collection, sadly moth-eaten. Viola's neighbor still patrols the halls in her curlers, loudly disapproving of Dot and Ralfie's visitors—especially the Tran family, Jim and Mai and Bao, who join them for the occasional Sunday brunch; but also Susan and Cynthia, back together and grabbing a brief smooch on the threshold before they ring the doorbell; Shawn, now a weekend dad dragging along his sullen adolescent twins, since Clarisse up and left him for his third cousin, the drummer in a country-and-western band; and Nelson and his boyfriend, who Nelson has finally stopped pretending is just a roommate.

In that future, Dot continues to occasionally find the ducky, which migrates into the pockets of various jackets and pants. It surprises her every time.

Acknowledgments

With much thanks for encouragement, good ideas, edits, and friendship: Robin Becker, Richard Burns, Jennifer Camper, Mary Cappello, Ineke Ceder, Kate Clinton, Anita Diamant, Stephen McCauley, Betsy Smith, Urvashi Vaid, Jean Walton; writer-colleagues at the Solstice Low-Residency MFA Program, including Anne-Marie Oomen and Meg Kearney; fellowships at the Virginia Center for Creative Arts and friends made there, including Natania Rosenfeld and Ruth Danon; University of Wisconsin Press director Dennis Lloyd, acquisitions assistant Jacqulyn Teoh, and senior project editor Sheila McMahon; my late, beloved, much-missed parents, Serena and Sigmund Hoffman; my family, including David Hoffman, Judith Hoffman, Priscilla Morrissey, Rebecca Hoffman, and Rachel Morrissey; the Provincetown Public Library; and my life-partner and love always, Roberta Stone.